La Puta Vida Trilogy

by Reinaldo Povod

Original New York Production by
New York Shakespeare Festival
Produced by Joseph Papp

A SAMUEL FRENCH ACTING EDITION

SAMUEL FRENCH
FOUNDED 1830

New York Hollywood London Toronto
SAMUELFRENCH.COM

IMPORTANT BILLING AND CREDIT REQUIREMENTS

All producers of LA PUTA VIDA *must* give credit to the Author of the Play in all programs distributed in connection with performances of the Play and in all instances in which the title of the Play appears for purposes of advertising, publicizing or otherwise exploiting the Play and/or a production. The name of the Author *must* also appear on a separate line, in which no other name appears, immediately following the title, and *must* appear in size of type not less than fifty percent the size of the title type.

IN ADDITION, the following *must* be included in all programs:

Original New York Production by
New York Shakespeare Festival.
Produced by Joseph Papp.

The Public/LuEsther Hall

A New York Shakespeare Festival Production

JOSEPH PAPP

presents

LA PUTA VIDA TRILOGY
THIS BITCH OF A LIFE

by
REINALDO POVOD

Directed by
BILL HART

with

RAFAEL BAEZ

MICHAEL CARMINE

MIGUEL CORREA

ROSANA DeSOTO

MICHAEL GUESS

JOHN LEGUIZAMO

JOHN TURTURRO

Scenery by
DONALD EASTMAN

Costumes by
GABRIEL BERRY

Lighting by
ANNE MILITELLO

Sound Designer/Composer
DANIEL MOSES SCHREIER

Casting by
ROSEMARIE TICHLER/NANCY PICCIONE

Associate Producer
JASON STEVEN COHEN

Prologue

Papo .... MICHAEL CARMINE

South of Tomorrow

Time: Fall, 1978

Lookout .... RAFAEL BAEZ
Alley Boy .... JOHN LEGUIZAMO
Randy .... MICHAEL GUESS

Nijinsky Choked His Chicken

Time: Summertime

Raisin .... MIGUEL CORREA
Chino .... JOHN TURTURRO

Poppa Dio!

Scene I: Autumn

Scene II: A few hours earlier

Angelo .... JOHN TURTURRO
Mafia .... ROSANA DeSOTO

Epilogue

Papo .... MICHAEL CARMINE

THERE WILL BE TWO TEN-MINUTE INTERMISSIONS.

UNDERSTUDIES
Understudies never substitute for listed players unless a specific announcement
for the appearance is made at the time of the performance.
For Michael Carmine and John Leguizamo—Rafael Baez;
for Miguel Correa—Rahshan Orange.

THE PROLOGUE

SCENE: *The LIGHTS RISE on the stage to reveal the playing area littered with empty cans of "Goya Beans," empty milk cartons, bottles of "Miller Beer," "El Diario." Newspaper is scattered about. Empty food stamp booklets lie where they have been thrown in disappointment.*

AT RISE: *The sounds of a BABY CRYING are heard faintly, and the VOICES of a man and a woman are heard loudly arguing in Spanish. A BUS PASSING by is heard. A MAN HAWKS: "Ups, downs, loose joints." A police SIREN is heard. CHILDREN LAUGHING. All come together and build to a climax.*

Silence.

A large empty glass candle will roll down the center of the stage. A YOUNG MAN will enter right behind it. HE has a cane and walks with a limp. He is lean and very handsome. Although he is in his mid- to late-twenties, his greatest charm is his boyishness. HE stares at the audience. He is dressed in dirty jeans, motorcycle boots, and wears a sleeveless denim jacket with a white fox collar over an ankle-length leather jacket. He has a nicely trimmed van-dyke on his face, and long shoulder-length hair.

PAPO. *(Touches his leg.)* Gun shot wound. A .22 went

7

clean through. Thank God. How'd I get it? How did I get
shot? On the subway. I was takin' this guy off in the subway — cowboying 'im — when I went for my piece.
Bang! I shot myself. Pulling it out, you know? No big
deal. It be's that way sometimes. As we take-off artists say.
Life ain't that important to me. What is important is how
it's affecting my mother. What I gotta do for me and her
to survive this Puta life. It hit me when I got shot. She
gotta heart condition and I can't let my Puta life do her in.
She's all I got. And I'm all she's got. And the saddest sight
in the world is a man without a mother. And worst, you
know, a mother without a son. Think about it. That's
hard, man, a mother who's no longer a mother — she's
no longer called a mother. 'Cause her kid don't exist —
ain't there for her — 'cept in her heart. She's jus' a broad,
nothin', that's all. My mother is in the hospital now —
gotta fifty-fifty chance. An' it's all because of this "Puta
Vida." I been with her 26 years — never missed a day not
being with her. And it never crossed my mind she not
being with me. Until the day I got outta the hospital.
Instead of going home to her — I spent ten hours in a
shootin' gallery. Ten hours shootin' coke. Ten fuckin'
hours. It was exactly six in the morning when I got outta.
the shootin' gallery. Something was sayin' to me, go
home, man, hurry up, go home. My arm was swollen
from hittin' myself all night. —An' every time I leaned on
the cane it hurt. I tried to walk as fast as I could. My heart
beating against my ribcage — from all the coke I shot up
and from fear. She's dead. I know. Yer gonna find her
dead. I am—. Hurry up, man. She's dead in the house —
alone. All by herself. Where were you? I know. She was

yours. Nobody else's. She belonged only to you. Where
were you? I know. In a shootin' gallery. Yeah. I was in a
shootin' gallery and she was alone, dying. We both were.
I opened my door. Cold. It was cold inside. I hate when
she sleeps on the sofa. I hate it, man. I don't like you
sleepin' on the sofa. That thin sheet — I hate that even
more — that thin white sheet all us poor ass Spanish people use to cover ourselves in the winter time. I saw her
deformed feet — pale with cold — and I wanted to cover
them with the white sheet. But I hate that white sheet! I
looked at her. Her thick snow white hair — I wanted to
touch it, smell it. Kiss her head. Ohh, man. I really did.
But I never touched my mother in that way. I'd kill
myself for her, but I can't, you know, touch her — that
way. That's me. I want to — I want to hold her in my arms
— I know a lot of sons do that — I dunno — I can't! I
looked at her — down at her chest — she's old — It hurts
me to see her breasts sag — weak. I seen pictures of her
when she was younger, man, those things were hard and
strong — I know God licked his chops everytime my
mother touched her breast in praise of his name. I put
my face right up to hers to see — I didn't want to. I wish I
didn't have to — 'cause if she suddenly woke up and
caught me worried — she'd make a big deal outta it 'an
embarrass me. I know she'd feel good, seeing me caring,
you know? But I'm the man. You know? The man of the
house — gotta be strong. She was hardly breathing,
man, my eyes swelled up — I couldn't breathe — All
of a sudden I wanted to lay down next to her — Like
maybe if I held on to her — I'd be able to go with
her — She'd take me with her. I ran to Cuca next

door — told her to call the ambulance. *(Long pause.)* She's in intensive care now. And I know she's gonna die. That's why I'm here. I know tonight, she's gonna die. In a few hours I'm gonna be motherless. And I'm gonna be angry. Hateful, angry. *(Long pause.)* In school, a teacher once asked me, "Raphael, why are you so full of hate? You're a hateful shild — you mustn't be that way." *(Long pause.)* I'm here... 'Cause if... When my mother dies — I'm gonna kill someone. I'm gonna use this cane to beat the anger outta me. I know. But I don't care. I gonna kill someone in a few hours. Has anyone here ever sat down with a Latino? A Latino like myself — and listened to him? *(Slowly, for effect.)* Listen to 'im... Because he has something to say. Lissen to 'im— Not — because he needs guidance, or assistance from you, you know, for food stamps, welfare, brother can you spare a dime. Lissen to 'im— Not — because you wanna hear him tell why he stabbed that one-hundred-and-ten-year-old woman in Soho. Forty times. Lissen to 'im— Not — because you hate Spiks, you hate and identify everything that is wrong, from pushing in the subways to child molestation with him. Lissen to 'im, because he is a man. And men do these things. And are gonna keep on doin' these things! Look at me. Look me up and down. I feel proud. I wouldn't be askin' you to check me out if I didn't feel proud. Dangerous. O.K., that's enough. I wanna give you all something. *(Takes a knife out.)* Awright, nobody move. Gimme all yer money! *(Pause.)* This is not what I wann give you. *(As he folds knife and puts it back in his pocket.)* I didn't want to let those of you out there who were expectin' something like this from me — I didn't wanna let yous down. *(Long pause.)* I don't know anymore. It makes me angry sometimes. Stereotypes. Us. And other times it makes me proud. Yeah, we're bad. We're surviving the ghettos. Not many can. Like the Warsaw Ghetto... I dunno, man. I know my mother dies — I know what I'm gonna do. I awready told you what. I don't care. And if she don't die — that's why I wrote this Trilogy. "La Puta Vida." I wanna put my "Puta Vida" up on stage. Step back and see this Puta world my mother and me live in from where yer sittin'. *(Long pause.)* What yer gonna see here are three one-act plays. It's more for me than for you people. You can go home afterwards. I can't. I have to stop. Stoppit all. I don't wanna hurt no one. I don't wanna hurt none of yous out there. I know. I'm gonna. If I don't stop. I'm gonna hurt myself too. If I don't put a stop to it. Please bear with me. Somehow. I feel, you know, this is selfish — what I'm doing here. But I need help. Stay here with me, O.K.? For a little while. At the end of the play you tell me what I'm suppose to do. *(Long pause.)* And if my mother dies? Run! 'Cause I swear to God, man. I'm gonna kill somebody. I don't care who. I dunno who? Maybe a mother, maybe a son... Like me... Help me, please. Or, please stop me. My thing ain't hurtin' people. *(HE slowly turns and walks away. The LIGHTS on stage will slowly dim out.)* But I don't want my mother to die. *(He sobs loudly.)* Oh, God. Don't let it. *(Sobs.)* No don't. *(Sobs.)*

SOUTH OF TOMORROW

CHARACTERS

RANDY: *A black man in his mid-thirties. A Vietnam War veteran. Wears a patch over his eye.*

ALLEY BOY: *A 17-year-old. Hispanic.*

OFF-STAGE: *A young raspy voice. Rough, from years of heroin abuse.*

SCENE: *A shooting gallery. A bare stage except for a plastic milk container filled with water, and a tin can of coffee filled with one hyperdermic syringe. And also a small coffee mug. Darkness.*

TIME: *Fall of 1978.*

OFF-STAGE VOICE. Redlight. Don't go in. Redlight. Cops coming down the block. La Jara, man, keep walkin'. Move, bro. No, nah, man, don't stand there. MOVE! YO?? YOU? Yeah!!

ALLEY BOY. *(Off.)* Sorry.

OFF-STAGE VOICE. Let the cops go by. Yeah. *(Long silence.)* Get in, c'mon, hurry up. Let's go! You slow bro.

ALLEY BOY. *(Off.)* Sorry.

OFF-STAGE VOICE. Git yer money out.

RANDY. *(Off.)* How much to git off?

OFF-STAGE VOICE. You got works?

RANDY. *(Off.)* I gotta "cooker."

OFF-STAGE VOICE. Three dollars. How 'bout you, bro?

ALLEY BOY. *(Off.)* ... Sorry.

OFF-STAGE VOICE. *(Upset.)* Sorry for what, bro?

ALLEY BOY. *(Off.)* Excuse me?

OFF-STAGE VOICE. Yo, man. Take a walk.

ALLEY BOY. *(Off.)* I'm sorry.

OFF-STAGE VOICE. Stupid guy like you — I can get busted for a stupid ass like you.

ALLEY BOY. *(Off.)* I'm sorry.

OFF-STAGE VOICE. Gimme three dollars. *(Annoyed.)* Gimme, c'mon, bro. What the fuck is this?

ALLEY BOY. *(Off.)* Three dollars.

RANDY. Man, can I go in? I awready paid you.

OFF-STAGE VOICE. Yeah.

(RANDY enters the stage.)

OFF-STAGE VOICE. This is a five, bro, I only take singles.

ALLEY BOY. *(Off.)* I'm sorry.

RANDY. Hey, mah man, there ain't no lights in here.

OFF-STAGE VOICE. Light a match — there's candles.

ALLEY BOY. *(Off.)* I'm sorry, I didn't know — here's the three dollars.

OFF-STAGE VOICE. See it? *(RANDY lights a match.)*

RANDY. Yeah. *(Proceeds to light the candles on stage.)*

OFF-STAGE VOICE. You in't coming in next time.

ALLEY BOY. *(Off.)* I'm sorry. Here. One. Two, three

dollars. I didn't know.

OFF-STAGE VOICE. Everybody knows — it's three dollars to git off in a shootin' gallery — you jus' slow, bro.

ALLEY BOY. *(Off.)* Sorry.

OFF-STAGE VOICE. In there.

ALLEY BOY. *(Off.)* In here?

OFF-STAGE VOICE. You deaf?

ALLEY BOY. *(Off.)* Sorry?

OFF-STAGE VOICE. Git the fuck in there.

(TEDDY enters the stage.)

ALLEY BOY. Ah, excuse me — but you still have my five dollars.

OFF-STAGE VOICE. You didn't gimme no five dollars.

ALLEY BOY. Yes I did. I gave you a five dollar bill.

OFF-STAGE VOICE. I ain't got it.

ALLEY BOY. Yes you do.

OFF-STAGE VOICE. Motherfucker, I said, I ain't got it. *(Shoves Alley Boy violently back onto the main playing area.)* Yo, man, don't come out till I say Green Light.

RANDY. Awright, man.

OFF-STAGE VOICE. Green Light.

ALLEY BOY. Green Light?

RANDY. Yeah, Green Light.

OFF-STAGE VOICE. Red Light—

ALLEY BOY. I thought you said — Green Light?

RANDY. Let 'im talk.

OFF-STAGE VOICE. Hey, stupid.

ALLEY BOY. Yes, I'm sorry. I'm sorry to interrupt.

RANDY. This guy - is gonna get us busted.

OFF-STAGE VOICE. You get me busted, bro, I'm gonna stab you.

ALLEY BOY. I'm sorry.

RANDY. Shut up, man. You a sorry dude - Shut up.

OFF-STAGE VOICE. Green Light - you come out. Red Light, you stay inside.

RANDY. I gotchu, brother man.

ALLEY BOY. Yes, thank you.

RANDY. Don't thank 'im, man.

ALLEY BOY. Yes, you're right. We're the victims.

RANDY. Huh?

ALLEY BOY. Nothing. *(pause)* Boy, it's the ante chamber to hell.

RANDY. What?

ALLEY BOY. It's the ante chamber to hell.

RANDY. Yeah. This place is South Of - Tomorrow.

ALLEY BOY. South of Tomorrow.

RANDY. Yeah. Like you said, "It's the ante chamber to hell."

ALLEY BOY. South of Tomorrow - I like that. *(RANDY takes one of the candles to look at the tin can of coffee to see how many hypodermics there are. seeing only one, HE becomes upset. Extremely angry.)*

RANDY. Ahh, shit, this can't be happening. No, man, nothin's right. Again?! God. Again from Poo nang - *(Slaps his thighs.)* All over, all over, all over. *(HE stops.)* It's foo nang all over again.

ALLEY BOY. Foo nang.

RANDY. Foo nang. Poo nang - It's Poo nang, all over again!

ALLEY BOY. That one I know 'cause you said it.

RANDY. Yeah, it's Foo Man Chu.

ALLEY BOY. *(To himself.)* Foo Man Chu, I know that name. Christopher Lee, right?

RANDY. *(Walking around, to himself.)* Poo nang, to Foo nang, to Foo Man Chu nang, to shit man!

ALLEY BOY. Shit man?

RANDY. To Danang.

ALLEY BOY. Ohh, shit, man, I got you...Vietnam!

RANDY. *(Long pause - to himself.)* That must be why these brothers out here tattoo on their arms - "Mi Vida Loca." Ain't no other way but to accept this shit and understand it a crazy life.

ALLEY BOY. What's wrong?

RANDY. I don't.

ALLEY BOY. What?

RANDY. I been singled out, B.

ALLEY BOY. I believe you.

RANDY. I have - man.

ALLEY BOY. Do you know for what?

RANDY. *(angry)* For what? For what? Use yer eyes - For what??

ALLEY BOY. Yes.

RANDY. Look.

ALLEY BOY. For what?

RANDY. We only got one set of works - only gimmicks.

ALLEY BOY. Be my guest. It's not a big deal.

RANDY. To me it is. *(RANDY prepares his shot of dope. Taps out the contents from his dime bag into his cooker. [Bottle Cap] Applies water. Heats. Withdraws the solution into the syringe. But*

now and then HE stops to talk to ALLEY BOY.) I got a bitch of
a habit.

ALLEY BOY. I don't have a habit.

RANDY. You don't know how lucky you are. You
bless.

ALLEY BOY. I only got what they call - I think - a
chippy?

RANDY. Lemme tell 'ya blood...Lemme hold 'ya hand.
Gimme yer hand for a second. *(ALLEY BOY does.)* Yeah. I
knew it. It's warm and real. *(Releases his hand.)* You know
what happened to me today? You know what they say
about a nigguh? Yeah, I'm a nigguh. Today I'm a nigguh
- today - anybody who goes into a shootin' gallery is a
nigguh - On other days - I am a "Negril" but today I'm a
dumb ass nigguh - You dig what I'm saying? I'm saying -
everybody says - a nigguh's cock - make a fist - like that.
Yeah. Everybody says - That's the head of a nigguh's
cock. Whadda you say?

ALLEY BOY. I say I envy you.

RANDY. It's true - It's true what they say we got b'tween
our legs.

ALLEY BOY. I believe you.

RANDY. You didn't know?

ALLEY BOY. No.

RANDY. You never saw one?

ALLEY BOY. Sorry.

RANDY. I won't show you mine.

ALLEY BOY. Thanks.

RANDY. But it's like that. *(Shows ALLEY BOY his fist.)*

ALLEY BOY. Yeah, you showed me.

RANDY. No. You missin' it. *(Shows ALLEY BOY his fist.)*

It's clenched full of pride. That's what these motherfuckers out here always leave out when they talk about a nigguh's cock. Pride.

ALLEY BOY. I always thought it was like a pepperoni stick. Italians are proud too. It's almost the same thing.

RANDY. *(Ties his arm with a belt.)* Today. I walked into a temp agency. Lookin' for work. This nigguh here, this proud Negril - said - Good morning. I wanna work. Please. Excuse me. Good morning. I wanna work - I say again to the receptionist. Please. She ignores me. Excuse me. I wanna work, please...Excuse me. Finally - she acknowledges this potentially but hard earned dangerous stare of mine. You know? She lowers her eyes the way she suppose to. "What have you been doing with yerself?" What have I been doing with myself? Man, I told this over-estimated bitch! "I want a job!" "But what experience do you have?" *(angry)* I spent two fucking years in the bush - two Jesus fucking Christ years, lady, in the bush. *(soft)* Now, ma'am, don't you think I can clean toilets? I heard her say when I tip'ed - "That guy got a problem." Me? I been out here on these streets, brother man, a long time - been here on this grinnin' face planet - feel like longer than mankind, yeah. But I never, man, never been humiliated like I was in that office. Out here on these streets, man - I been physically abuse, been verbally abuse - but never been degraded. *(Shoot up his heroin. Long silence.)* Here. *(Give ALLEY BOY the hypodermic.)* Clean 'im - clean 'im good before you use them. This 3-star dope - is bullshit. It settled my stomach - but it didn't get me high. Ain't that some shit.

ALLEY BOY. ...Can I see your eye?

RANDY. What did you say? Did you say - you wanna see my eye?

ALLEY BOY. Yes.

RANDY. *(laughs)* Holy shit. Am I suppose to be impressed, or something?

ALLEY BOY. No, of course not.

RANDY. You wanna surprise me with yer skinny ass se'f?

ALLEY BOY. No, I don't.

RANDY. Whachu think you lookin' at?

ALLEY BOY. ...I'm lookin' at you.

RANDY. Right. *(shouts)* Yo? I'm comin' out!

ALLEY BOY. Don't go.

OFF-STAGE VOICE. Red Light - stay inside.

RANDY. You lookin' at my eye, fool.

ALLEY BOY. I know.

RANDY. It's the eye I ain't got you wanna check out.

ALLEY BOY. Yes - if you don't mind.

RANDY. What s'matter? - This here one eye bores the shit outta yer tight ass self?

ALLEY BOY. No.

RANDY. You wanna freak out on the one - got pop'd outta my head - and buried in the ground - like a dog burying his bone.

ALLEY BOY. No.

RANDY. No. Shut the fuck up with them no's. That all you can say?

ALLEY BOY. *(pause)* No.

RANDY. No.

ALLEY BOY. I'm sorry.

RANDY. That too - I don't wanna hear anymore no's or I'm sorry's outta you. You dig what I'm saying, B?

ALLEY BOY. I do.

RANDY. You think it takes courage to ask me something like that?

ALLEY BOY. ...No.

RANDY. Don't wanna hear any no's.

ALLEY BOY. I'm sorry.

RANDY. Don't wanna hear that trash either.

ALLEY BOY. I don't know what to say then.

RANDY. Nothin'.

ALLEY BOY. You're wrong.

RANDY. Don't tell me I'm wrong.

ALLEY BOY. I'm—

RANDY. Don't say sorry.

ALLEY BOY. I won't.

RANDY. ...You think rejecting something - something like me - an evil, nasty lookin' one eye monster...

ALLEY BOY. No - You're wrong.

RANDY. What did I tell you?

ALLEY BOY. I don't know how else to say it - when you're wrong.

RANDY. You think it takes courage—

ALLEY BOY. No.

RANDY. Lemme finish - motherfucker. You think it takes courage to look me in my empty socket an' say, "It ain't shit."

ALLEY BOY. No.

RANDY. (angry) Don't tell me no!

ALLEY BOY. I don't wanna reject life.

RANDY. You wanna be envied?

ALLEY BOY. How?

RANDY. To ast to look at something that best remain behind curtains, ignored an' shit - is to be envied. 'Specially if you're askin' a nigguh. Nobody ever asts a person who gotta patch over his eye can he see the nasty thing. What? You wanna rub it for good luck? Or, are you one of these - you know - them morbid freaks? - Do yer shit, man, and leave my eye alone.

ALLEY BOY. ...I don't have any dope.

RANDY. You don't have any shit?!

ALLEY BOY. I don't have any dope.

RANDY. How 'bout coke?

ALLEY BOY. Nothin'.

RANDY. Nothin'? Wachu doin' in a shootin' gallery if you ain't got no shit to shoot up? *(long pause)* What kinda freak are you?

ALLEY BOY. Don't get angry - please, I'm not a freak. *(RANDY grabs Alley Boy in a full-nelson.)* Please leave me alone.

RANDY. *(Walks Alley Boy over to the candles - bends him forward.)* Grab one of 'em candles. *(ALLEY BOY does.)* Gimme it. Gimme it, man. *(ALLEY BOY hands it to him. RANDY releases him.)* Lemme see some trackmarks. *(RANDY grabs Alley Boy by his shirt and menaces him with the candle.)* I'll put yer hair on fire. *(ALLEY BOY rolls his sleeves up.)* Nothin' -Nothin' man - You ain't a junkie. *(shouts)* Hey, man, lemme outta here.

OFF-STAGE VOICE. ...Be cool - Red Light. Cops parked outside.

ALLEY BOY. How did you lose yer eye?

RANDY. Look man, I ain't no freak.

ALLEY BOY. No. I know you're not.

RANDY. Ast me my name - don't ast me that kind'ah thing.

ALLEY BOY. What's your name?

RANDY. Randy.

ALLEY BOY. Nice to meet you, Randy. I'm Alley Boy.

RANDY. Alley Boy.

ALLEY BOY. Yes.

RANDY. Why?

ALLEY BOY. Why am I called Alley Boy?

RANDY. Yeah, why?

ALLEY BOY. I don't know - that's my nickname.

RANDY. Nickname, huh. who gave you this nickname?

ALLEY BOY. People.

RANDY. People, huh. What kinda people?

ALLEY BOY. People, that's all. People.

RANDY. People who live in alleys?

ALLEY BOY. No.

RANDY. People who shoot up in alleys?

ALLEY BOY. No.

RANDY. People who rob people in alleys?

ALLEY BOY. No.

RANDY. People who take li'l girls and li'l boys into alleys?

ALLEY BOY. No.

RANDY. And fuck them???

ALLEY BOY. *(shouts)* No!

OFF-STAGE VOICE. Yo - Be cool in there. Cops are out here.

RANDY. People who kill people in alleys?

ALLEY BOY. *(long pause)* No.

RANDY. That kinda people, right? Yeah.

ALLEY BOY. No.

RANDY. What kind of people are you?

ALLEY BOY. ...No kind.

RANDY. Nah, you're the worst kind. You scare me.

ALLEY BOY. No.

RANDY. Yeah, man. You the kind - the kind that gets off on askin' a kid if he got a chance to see his mother get run over by the train.

ALLEY BOY. No, Randy, that's not me.

RANDY. Did he really see the wheels roll over her neck?

ALLEY BOY. That's horrible - Randy, don't say that. C'mon, man.

RANDY. You'd probably ast him did he maybe see her head roll. Can he maybe show you the spot where it happened.

ALLEY BOY. I wouldn't do that.

RANDY. You'd do more.

ALLEY BOY. I'm not that kind.

RANDY. You'd wanna go down and stare at the blood.

ALLEY BOY. No. No. No.

RANDY. Yes. Yes. Yes.

ALLEY BOY. *(Lifts his hands as if to strike Randy.)* NO!

RANDY. *(Challenges him.)* Shut the fuck up!

ALLEY BOY. ...I'm like you.

RANDY. *(pause)* Nah.

ALLEY BOY. I am. Please, Randy, believe me. I am.

RANDY. ...Yo? Is it cool out there yet?

OFF-STAGE VOICE. Stay inside. Red Light.

ALLEY BOY. You - you lost yer eye.

RANDY. Fuck my eye.

ALLEY BOY. You got nothin' to lose.

RANDY. You deaf, man?

ALLEY BOY. ...'Cept yer other eye.

RANDY. You crazy?

ALLEY BOY. You're like me - I'm like you. I got nothin'
to lose. Serious, Randy, I don't.

RANDY. *(shouts)* Yo?

OFF-STAGE VOICE. Shut up - Red Light.

RANDY. Shut up, man awright? Shut yer mouth - I
don't wanna hear it.

ALLEY BOY. ...I followed you.

RANDY. Say what?

ALLEY BOY. I saw you.

RANDY. You saw me where?

ALLEY BOY. Walking.

RANDY. Walking? Scouting for a bag - you mean?

ALLEY BOY. I followed you.

RANDY. ...What do you want?

ALLEY BOY. I saw you.

RANDY. Yeah, I know, you followed me.

ALLEY BOY. I want to give you something.

RANDY. What do you wanna give me?

ALLEY BOY. Something.

RANDY. Don't play games with me, B.

ALLEY BOY. Lemme see your eye.

RANDY. How much you gonna give me?

ALLEY BOY. It's not money.

RANDY. I need money.

ALLEY BOY. You don't need money.

RANDY. You got money?

ALLEY BOY. Yes. But that's not what you need.

RANDY. Gimme some money - man.

ALLEY BOY. Sure...Here.

RANDY. *(takes it)* Ten dollars. A bag of dope. that all you got?

ALLEY BOY. It's all I got.

RANDY. Empty yer pockets out. *(ALLEY BOY does.)* You got any jewelry?

ALLEY BOY. Sorry.

RANDY. Not even a watch?

ALLEY BOY. You don't need a watch - Randy.

RANDY. I need a watch. Money. And pussy.

ALLEY BOY. I got candy.

RANDY. Candy - what kind?

ALLEY BOY. Reese's peanut butter cups.

RANDY. Nah. I like Milky Ways. Frozen.

RANDY. Yo, man, what's happening out there?

ALLEY BOY. The money is nothin' compared to what I have for you.

RANDY. You told me you ain't got no jewelry.

ALLEY BOY. Yes, I know. I don't.

RANDY. You best not be jiving me.

ALLEY BOY. You can check me.

RANDY. Normally I would - but with you - I don't know about you. Siddown man, and stop pulling   my Johnson.

ALLEY BOY. Tell me about yer eye.

RANDY. Dag boy...

ALLEY BOY. I said tell me about it - not show it to me.

RANDY. *(long pause)* Awright. I got yer ten dollars - I guess it's awright.

ALLEY BOY. Can I...

RANDY. Can you what?

ALLEY BOY. Can I come over there to you?

RANDY. *(upset)* I'm gonna go off on you, man, you makin' my stomach turn. Commere, man, I'm gonna tell you something. Commere. I ain't gonna go off on you - I just wanna check you out. *(Quickly grabs a candle.)* I don't go for intimidation - That don't go with me - Nobody intimidates me - I intimidate them - Are you down on what I'm saying?

ALLEY BOY. I don't think I'm intimidating.

RANDY. I don't know about you - man.

ALLEY BOY. Tell me about your eye - Randy?

RANDY. *(angry)* STOP! *(Grabs Alley Boy and smacks him a few times on the side of his head, saying:)* Motherfucker, stop, stop, motherfucker! *(ALLEY BOY removes his patch. RANDY is startled. HE stops hitting Alley Boy and remains motionless - glaring at Alley Boy.)*

ALLEY BOY. *(long pause)* Here. *(long pause)* I'm sorry. *(Extends Randy's eye patch out to him.)*

RANDY. No. No.

ALLEY BOY. Don't you wanna put it back on?

RANDY. You took it offa me.

ALLEY BOY. I did. I'm sorry. *(long pause)* Do you want me to put it back on you? Is that it?

RANDY. *(Awkward silence. Forcefully, RANDY takes hold of Alley Boy's head and jerks it back violently. Almost pressing his*

own face against Alley Boy - nose to nose - he says to Alley Boy.)
You evil - man. You an evil dude.

ALLEY BOY. No, I'm not - Randy. Please.

RANDY. I can see it in yer eyes.

ALLEY BOY. You're mistaken, Randy.

RANDY. I feel it. I feel it coming outta you, man.

ALLEY BOY. No. My eyes are kind.

RANDY. Shit.

ALLEY BOY. They are, Randy. They really are.

RANDY. Kind - shit!

ALLEY BOY. Once you got 'em.

RANDY. ...What?!

ALLEY BOY. They'll become—

RANDY. What?

ALLEY BOY. Kind.

RANDY. ...What did you say? Say what you said all over again.

ALLEY BOY. *(long pause)* That's what I have in mind to give you.

RANDY. Your eyes?

ALLEY BOY. Yes.

RANDY. *(Releases Alley Boy.)* ...Whatta 'bout you?

ALLEY BOY. Nothing.

RANDY. Huh?

ALLEY BOY. I won't need 'em.

RANDY. You won't need 'em? Everybody needs their eyes!

ALLEY BOY. I won't need 'em.

RANDY. Why - what's wrong with 'em?

ALLEY BOY. Nothing.

RANDY. 20 -20?

ALLEY BOY. Yes.

RANDY. What color?

ALLEY BOY. Brown.

RANDY. Beautiful.

ALLEY BOY. They are?

RANDY. ...Who are you, man?

ALLEY BOY. ...I'm not what you think.

RANDY. A freak?

ALLEY BOY. No.

RANDY. Crazy?

ALLEY BOY. No.

RANDY. You jus' gonna gimme yer eyes - like that.

ALLEY BOY. After you tell me some things about yourself.

RANDY. Are you messin' wit my head?

ALLEY BOY. No - I'm not messin' wit yer head.

RANDY. You gonna put this all on paper?

ALLEY BOY. Afterwards - yes.

RANDY. After what?

ALLEY BOY. *(slowly for effect)* After you tell me how you lost yer eye.

RANDY. How you gonna go about giving yer eyes to me?

ALLEY BOY. I'm gonna kill myself.

RANDY. *(smiling)* You gonna kill yourself?

ALLEY BOY. Yes, I am.

RANDY. When?

ALLEY BOY. Afterwards.

RANDY. After you write - saying you donate yer eyes to me?

ALLEY BOY. Afterwards.

RANDY. You're gonna kill yerself in front of me?

ALLEY BOY. Maybe.

RANDY. How?

ALLEY BOY. How - doesn't matter - I'm just gonna, okay?

RANDY. For me.

ALLEY BOY. For you. Or, for somebody more deserving than you.

RANDY. I never had nobody kill themselves for me.

ALLEY BOY. Were you born—

RANDY. Without my eye?

ALLEY BOY. Yes.

RANDY. No.

ALLEY BOY. You lost it in the War.

RANDY. Yeah, man. Covering some turkey's back.

ALLEY BOY. Good. Good.

RANDY. Say what?!

ALLEY BOY. It was a sacrifice.

RANDY. It was bullshit. It was an eye for an eye.

ALLEY BOY. An eye for an eye, yeah?

RANDY. Mine went South of Tomorrow. It waiting for me right now—

ALLEY BOY. I don't understand - Randy?

RANDY. You ain't bullshittin' me about nothin'?

ALLEY BOY. No, I'm not.*(Takes out his wallet - seraches for a card. Finds it and hands it to Randy.)* Read this.

RANDY. *(Takes the card and reads aloud.)* Uniform donor card. Robert Martinez. That's you?

ALLEY BOY. That's my name - yeah.

RANDY. In the hope I may help others, I hereby make this anatomical gift, if medically accepted, to take effect upon my death. The words and marks below indicate my desires. I give...You marked A.

ALLEY BOY. Yeah. Any needed organs or parts. *(long pause)*

RANDY. Man, you are weird.

ALLEY BOY. O.K. Take your time.

RANDY. You a scary dude. *(A long silence.)*

ALLEY BOY. I'm not, Randy.

RANDY. Why you wanna kill yerself for? You young. How old are you?

ALLEY BOY. 17.

RANDY. Seventeen? You got the whole world to kick around at that age.

ALLEY BOY. I know I'm not gonna accomplish anything.

RANDY. Accomplish wha?? You haven't even started. You still a cub.

ALLEY BOY. I jus' know I'm not. I can feel I'm not gonna do nothing.

RANDY. Have kids.

ALLEY BOY. That ain't...gonna satisfy me.

RANDY. Man, you chumpin' yerself.

ALLEY BOY. ...I can predict.

RANDY. You can see into the future.

ALLEY BOY. Only mine - I always could. I could always see ahead what was in store for me...But...I could only predict the worst. I could never make a prediction that was good come out for me. I've tried. I tried even against my better judgement - I went head on - 110 percent and still fuckin' failed.

RANDY. At what - brother man?

ALLEY BOY. You name it - Anything that had to do with something good happening to me - that could benefit me and my mother - I tried it. How can you have hope when you keep experiencing the worst?

RANDY. I don't know, man, you jus' don't think about those things.

ALLEY BOY. Why not?

RANDY. You're not suppose to.

ALLEY BOY. Then who is suppose to think about those things - evaluate 'em?

RANDY. I don't know - but I know Bellevue is full of 'em.

ALLEY BOY. Yeah, you know, I believe you. They're there - those people are there 'cause they did not only what I'm doing but they went and brought it up close to their eyes - and kept it there - I know - I know what you're saying. I know what I'm saying - Living a life is enough - but bringin' it up to the eyes is crazy - I know I can go crazy. I know. I feel I can. I felt it a lot of times. 'Cause having brought it up close to my eyes - I can see certain things more clearly - and that can frighten me. That's why I'm here. *(long pause)* How 'bout it, Randy? Am I still a scary dude?

RANDY. You sound confuse.

ALLEY BOY. But I know what I wanna do. And that brings us back to you.

RANDY. Awright, mah man, I'm gonna lay it on to you. I'm gonna play this out wit 'ya.

OFF-STAGE VOICE. Red Light. Stay inside. Cops parked outside.

RANDY. *(long pause)* I never told this to anyone.

ALLEY BOY. Sure you have.

RANDY. I have, huh?

ALLEY BOY. You like talkin' about it.

RANDY. *(upset)* To who?

ALLEY BOY. To yerself.

RANDY. Man, git off it. *(long pause)* I had one slip up down here.

ALLEY BOY. Only one?

RANDY. One, chump, one. If I had two, I would say two...or three, or four, awright?

ALLEY BOY. Sure, Randy.

RANDY. *(long pause)* My platoon was at point...And way up ahead - I saw this village. We all agreed we'd check it out b'fore breakin' for lunch. The only people I saw in this village were a bunch of ol' men in straw hats - Grandpappies. - An' these broads - man, that looked like they been laid, relayed, and parlayed - these broads - stand there in the doorway breast-feeding their babies - you know, like nothin'. Well. On this fucking day - One of these broads comes running at us - hauling ass - like a brother with a T.V. set - running for dear life. My lieutenant shouts at 'er, "Dug Lai cunt, Dung Lai, you skank!" Halt. Halt, she could be booby trap. Blow her away, I said. Blow the mother away. What the fuck are you doing, man? This sonavabitch is holding hands with her. "Where you going, Lieutenant?" Boom Boom house. The Boom Boom house. You know, the whore house. The bitch was a 'ho. Just gonna get me a little poon-tang - shit, this man would stick his dick into a key-hole. I squatted down like this - waited for my lieutenant to tame his thing, you know? An' I...I stared down at this dry stream bed that led up a hill. Weird how, you know, you can remember that kinda thing - show me a stream bed now and I'd probably step in it and not know I'm in a fucking stream bed. *(Abruptly - blurts out sharply.)* Pop, pop, pop. I heard. Pop, pop, pop, pop-pop-pop!!! I made a beeline to the hut - the whorehouse, you know? An' man, my lieutenant. *(HE laughs.)* It ain't funny. But it's funny. This bad boy got whacked in one of the worst one of the most painful places a man can get hit. You know what I'm talkin' about, right?

ALLEY BOY. No.

RANDY. You a virgin, mah man?

ALLEY BOY. No.

RANDY. Yeah. *(HE is skeptical.)* You don't know whacha gonna be missin'. Piece of ass does wonders for yer mind - You heard a mind is a terrible thing to waste? A piece of ass is a crime not to have.

ALLEY BOY. Okay, yeah. But what happen to your lieutenant?

RANDY. You a Rican - right?

ALLEY BOY. Yes - I am.

RANDY. Where is the center of a Rican's man's pride?

ALLEY BOY. His heart.

RANDY. His heart?

ALLEY BOY. Yeah.

RANDY. You ain't Rican. Where's the Rican in you?

ALLEY BOY. I told you, in my heart.

RANDY. Machismo - brother man.

ALLEY BOY. Ohh - that. Shit.

RANDY. If you had that shit brother man - you'd be

kicking ass - instead of givin' it up. **Balls - brother man -
balls.** The center where a swift kick from the li'l lady you
were planning a rooftop lay with was called on account
she crippled yer peter. Balls - where - brother man,
sometimes deep love is erected and harden. My
lieutenant's balls caught two 7.62 mm bullets. Everybody gets what's coming to them. One brother Marine,
man. He emptied his magazine on the whore - inserted
another magazine - banged away again. Pop-pop-pop-
pop! We took everybody - kids, dogs, ol' men - them
Grandpappies I was tellin' ya about...All the whores, cats.
Chickens - we put 'em all in the Boom Boom house.
Don't come out we told them. Stay. Stay. Sit. Sit. Nice.
Nice. I...*(long pause)* I said - fuck 'em.

ALLEY BOY. Why?

RANDY. Why?

ALLEY BOY. Did you really feel something for your
superior?

RANDY. Superior shit. He was a jive-ass dude.

ALLEY BOY. So?

RANDY. So what?!

ALLEY BOY. The people - why did you say fuck 'em?

RANDY. I took my pack of matches - opened it like
this.

ALLEY BOY. Lemme see, Randy.

RANDY. *(Shows it to him.)* Took the cigarette outta my
mouth like this...Put it behind the matches - near the tips
of the matches, you know? Told my Platoon to keep
walkin'. Took this, you know, stuck it up in the corner of
the hut. So when the cigarette burns down to the tips of
the matches—

ALLEY BOY. The pack of matches lights up—

RANDY. —and sets fire to the hut. Yeah. In minutes that hut is in flames.

ALLEY BOY. What did you do then?

RANDY. Nothing.

ALLEY BOY. How did you feel? Burnin' them people up alive.

RANDY. An eye for an eye.

ALLEY BOY. *(long pause)* And your eye?

RANDY. Yeah, my eye what?!

ALLEY BOY. ...Did...did - did you have it?

RANDY. I had both my eyes when I saw the hut go up in flames. *(pause)* I lost it later on, a few seconds later, when the hut exploded. I got hit wit' some fragments.

ALLEY BOY. An eye for an eye.

RANDY. *(long pause)* What's it gonna be, Alley Cat?

ALLEY BOY. Robert.

RANDY. Robert. No. Alley Boy. You still a boy. You owe me something now - don't you?! *(long pause)* DON'T YOU?!

OFF-STAGE VOICE. Green Light. Come on out!

RANDY. Talk to me - man - 'cause I'm gonna jack you up.

ALLEY BOY. I haven't lied to you, Randy.

RANDY. What have you done to me? Man - c'mon.

OFF-STAGE VOICE. Green Light - Let's go.

RANDY. I didn't wanna believe you.

ALLEY BOY. I'm tellin' the truth.

RANDY. Boy come up to me with some off the wall jive about how he's gonna give me his eyes - I gotta be off the wall - stupid an' shit - to think - yeah...yeah.

ALLEY BOY. It's true.

RANDY. You gonna gimme yer eyes?

ALLEY BOY. No.

OFF-STAGE VOICE. *(Randy advances at Alley Boy but stops when HE hears:)* Green Light!

RANDY. *(shouts back)* Wait!

OFF-STAGE VOICE. Wait? Wait for what?

RANDY. You wait.

OFF-STAGE VOICE. It gonna cost you another three.

RANDY. You wait - man. You wait!

ALLEY BOY. I'm gonna take my life, Randy.

RANDY. I don't believe you—

ALLEY BOY. I will.

RANDY. Do it.

ALLEY BOY. Not now.

RANDY. You said you was. When? When, man?

ALLEY BOY. When I find someone - more deserving than you!

RANDY. What?! *(Advances at Alley Boy.)*

ALLEY BOY. You lost your eye - I can see why.

RANDY. Who you? God? You God?!

ALLEY BOY. YES.

RANDY. Say what?!

ALLEY BOY. Yes - I am God.

RANDY. Goddamn you then.

ALLEY BOY. I am God over my life.

RANDY. Goddamn you! Goddamn you! Goddamn YOU!

OFF-STAGE VOICE. Stop cursing God in there.

ALLEY BOY. I'm gonna give life to someone. A heart for someone to live. A liver for a child. My eyes to someone who has never done harm to anyone. Yes - Randy - I am God - But over my life.

RANDY. *(shouts)* Green Light out there?

OFF-STAGE VOICE. Stay inside. Red Light.

RANDY. *(angry)* Shit! *(pause)* I'm not deserving?

ALLEY BOY. ...No.

RANDY. God says no. No, I'm not.

ALLEY BOY. I say no.

RANDY. That's what I said. You.

ALLEY BOY. Yes.

RANDY. God. *(awkward silence)* The damnin' God - you - says. No. I'm not deserving.

ALLEY BOY. Yes.

RANDY. *(long pause)* Well, what happens when the God damnin' God you comes face to face with the real God Almighty?

ALLEY BOY. *(slowly, for effect)* I will give him my back. *(normal tone)* And - jump straight down into the fires of Hell.

RANDY. *(shouts)* Green Light?

ALLEY BOY. Red Light.

RANDY. You always been like this?

ALLEY BOY. Yes.

RANDY. Always?

ALLEY BOY. From the cradle.

RANDY. You got friends?

ALLEY BOY. People who are full of themselves - I don't want.

RANDY. You got friends?

ALLEY BOY. I got...No.

RANDY. You want friends?

ALLEY BOY. *(long pause)* Yes.

RANDY. You got a girlfriend?

ALLEY BOY. I could have.

RANDY. Yeah. You said you got beautiful brown eyes - I believe you there.

ALLEY BOY. I got you.

RANDY. Me?

ALLEY BOY. Now.

RANDY. I can't be your girlfriend.

ALLEY BOY. No - I know. I could be yours.

RANDY. Girlfriend??

ALLEY BOY. No - only friend.

RANDY. But I don't like you.

ALLEY BOY. That's right - I forgot.

RANDY. Besides - you suppose to kill yerself.

ALLEY BOY. I will.

RANDY. That thing you said about God...

ALLEY BOY. Do you blame God for anything?

RANDY. Nah, man.

ALLEY BOY. How come?

RANDY. If I could I would. But he's too complicated to pinpoint.

ALLEY BOY. I blame 'im.

RANDY. For the way you are?

ALLEY BOY. No. I like myself. Thank God for the way I am.

RANDY. I'm lost, man. Besides crazy. I am definitely lost.

ALLEY BOY. I blame 'im for the way others are. Where is God? Where is God? You know, Randy? I don't want nobody saying where was you - where was I? Here am I. I

got nothin' to offer - no money. No high school educa-
tion. No breaks. Nada. But me. An' before I go down,
you know - shootin' drugs, robbing people. Get involve
in that sort of life - where it becomes too late for me to
give - give my organs - 'cause I wanna give it - not 'cause I
wanna escape a fifteen to life sentence - so I kill myself -
I'm gonna do it now. And I wanna live - I wanna live,
Randy - I wanna live, I wanna live.

RANDY. *(long pause)* Here's yer ten dollars.

ALLEY BOY. Keep it - it's yours.

RANDY. Here, take it back.

ALLEY BOY. Why?

RANDY. I don't know why. I don't want it. There's
something about you. *(Finds it hard to say.)* Something
good.

ALLEY BOY. Thank you.

RANDY. Something cuckoo good about you.

OFF-STAGE VOICE. Green Light. Come out. Hurry
up.

RANDY. What are you gonna do?

ALLEY BOY. When?

RANDY. Now.

OFF-STAGE VOICE. Green Light - Come out.

ALLEY BOY. I don't know.

RANDY. You can't stay here—

ALLEY BOY. I give 'im another three dollars I can.

RANDY. And do what?

ALLEY BOY. I don't know.

RANDY. How was you gonna take yer life?

ALLEY BOY. Pills.

RANDY. Pills - lemme see 'em.

ALLEY BOY. *(Hands Randy a bottle.)* I got 40 sleepin' pills in there.

RANDY. You'd need a gallon of water to chug these suckers down.

ALLEY BOY. I don't need water to swallow pills.

RANDY. I could never do that. I need two glasses of water for one aspirin.

OFF-STAGE VOICE. Green Light - Git yer asses outta there - or, I'm gonna start chargin' yous.

RANDY. Don't do it.

ALLEY BOY. Huh?

RANDY. Lissen. Lissen to me. I'm always on the streets - I sleep right around here in an abandon building. Maybe...I don't know - you know?

ALLEY BOY. I told you we were both the same.

RANDY. You can help me by you know, maybe, bringin' me some food.

ALLEY BOY. All right.

RANDY. A blanket - it gets cold - you know. Then you know - in the meantime - you knows, you might meet - a nice chick.

ALLEY BOY. I don't know.

RANDY. You're a virgin, right? You haven't wet your beak - C'mon now, be honest? Awright then, whatever. - I use to be pretty - yeah - so I can teach everything I know.

OFF-STAGE VOICE. GREEN LIGHT.

RANDY. The nice - thing about suicide - brother man - you can put the sucker off - to a rainy day.

ALLEY BOY. That's true.

RANDY. There's always tomorrow.

ALLEY BOY. But not South.

RANDY. Hell, no.

ALLEY BOY. And today.

RANDY. You live another day.

OFF-STAGE VOICE. *(Enters the stage. Stands in the shadows.)* C'mon, let's go. Get outta here. *(Walks over to the candles. Blows them out.)*

BLACKOUT

NIJINSKY CHOKED
HIS CHICKEN

CHARACTERS

CHINO: *Late twenties. Hispanic. Sharp, distinct speech and quick, virile mind. Wears a nicely trimmed Van Dyke. He is tall and looks emaciated.*

RAISIN: *12-year-old boy. Sturdy, handsome.*

SCENE: *Raisin's apartment. The South Bronx.*

> *The kitchen—small. One single window, curtainless, shade-less, stands in the center of the stage—it is open. Weariness has, in fact, stamped itself in this kitchen, yellowing from years of grime and stained with cooking grease. Small kitchen table stands in the center. To the Right of it—near the window—is the customary stove. Stubborn. Will most likely still be there long after the occupants are dead and buried. Opposite this stove—alongside the window but on its Left—selected with care, actually bought and paid for second-hand—is the refrigerator. On top of this refrigerator—like the scarecrow in the fields— stands the two-foot statue of the "Sacred Heart of Jesus."*

TIME: *Summertime.*

AT RISE: *The sounds of CONGA DRUMS are heard beating with*

beautiful rhythm. Mid-afternoon. RAISIN wears his mother's apron over his white tee-shirt, jeans and sneakers. HE is sweeping the kitchen floor, lost in concentration. As RAISIN passes the window, HE stops sweeping, glances out. Enjoying the fast even pace the Conga players have taken.

OFF-STAGE VOICE (MALE). Did you spit?
RAISIN. Me?
OFF-STAGE VOICE (MALE). Did you spit?
RAISIN. No, I didn't spit.
OFF-STAGE VOICE (MALE). Who — spit me — man..
RAISIN. I didn't spit you.
OFF-STAGE VOICE (FEMALE). That's bird shit, bro...
RAISIN. *(Angered, RAISIN steps back from the window. To himself.)* I didn't spit nobody. *(Fiercely, he lunges towards the window again and spits, stepping back immediately.)*
OFF-STAGE VOICE (MALE). Yo?!
OFF-STAGE VOICE (FEMALE). It's bird shit.
OFF-STAGE VOICE (MALE). Dag, again?!

(RAISIN giggles. Takes his broom and resumes sweeping. Enjoying the sounds of the CONGAS. HE will take the telephone bill from the refrigerator. HE removes the bill and uses the envelope as a dust pan to scoop up the dirt from his floor. HE will dump his trash out the window. The broom, HE will return to its place near the side of the stove. HE will then take a seat at the kitchen table, facing the window, where HE will begin to bang on the table— playing along with the congas. HE will do this until he exhausts himself, knowing he cannot keep up with the rhythm. The sounds of the CONGAS will continue to fill his kitchen with their wonderful

sound. RAISIN will situate his seat— facing the audience. HE will stare out at them lost in thought. After some time HE will abruptly spring to his feet and exit the stage. Returning shortly thereafter with a Playboy magazine, HE will resume his seat at the kitchen table, devouring the magazine. RAISIN will stop turning the pages and will focus his attention on one page. Licking his lips in delight, HE will place the magazine on the table and will stand up to remove his pants. He allows them to drop down to his ankles. Next HE will slip his underwear down to his ankles. Next HE will resume his seat and will begin to masturbate, glancing over the Playboy magazine. Feeling self-conscious, HE will stop and turn his seat around, where now his back is towards the audience. HE will continue with his masturbation. Glancing around and up, HE will notice the statue of the "Sacred Heart of Jesus" glaring down on him. HE will stand and turn this statue around so the statue is not facing him, HE will take the dish rag and cover the statue with it. HE resumes his seat quickly, and proceeds to masturbate when suddenly HE stops.)

RAISIN. (Shouts.) Ouch! Ouch, (Stands and paces.) Ouch, ouch, ouch, (With his back to the audience he lifts his apron and looks down at himself.) Oh, God. Am I in trouble. (Shouts.) Blood! I'm bleeding to death. Oh, God. My pee-pee is bleeding. Oh, God. Help me. (Grabs the cloth he used to cover the statue of the "Sacred Heart of Jesus" with and will proceed to wipe himself. Wipe his penis.) Blood. (HE flings the rag out the window.)

OFF-STAGE VOICE (MALE). Yo? Hey? Who had their period?

RAISIN. (Frantic, HE puts his underwear and pants back on.) What do I do now—God? I'm bleeding to death. I'm gonna die. I knew it. My mo'her told me. Why didn't I lissen to her. I shoulda lissen'd to my mother - Oh, wow...There's blood on the floor - my mother will kill me. I got blood on the floor. Where's the rag? - I threw the rag out the window. The mop? Yeah, the mop. Where's the mop? We ain't got a mop. Jus' the rag. An' I threw the rag out the window. *(Long pause as he stares down at the blood. Sits on the floor and with his backside he wipes the blood clean off the floor. HE stands on his feet.)* My pants - I'll really get it now. I wonder if I stopped bleeding? *(RAISIN lifts his apron.)* Lemme see. *(Unzippers his pants, drops them and his underwear. Scrutinizes his privates, with his back towards the audience, says:)* Oh, no, I'm still bleeding. *(Puts his underwear and pants back on.)* This is what I get. Punishment. *(Speaks to the statue.)* Jesus, please. Please, Jesus. *(Notices the statue is not facing him. HE turns it around to face him.)* Please, Jesus. I'll never do this again. I promise Jesus. Take away the bleeding and I'll be good. I'll never play with myself again. I promise. Oh, Sacred Heart of Jesus, I consecrate my heart and soul to thee. I do. I do. I do. Really. Really, Jesus - man. C'mon, don't be like that. *(long pause)* I'm losing a lot of blood. I can die - here, you know? That's what I get for playing wit' myself. Man! I shoulda stopped. I didn't have to do it - I did it this morning. MAN. Whatta dope - I am. *(Crosses over to the window.)* Chino?! Chino?! Chino, man?!!

CHINO. Who callin' me?

RAISIN. Me - Chino - me.

CHINO. Where you at?

RAISIN. I'm here.

CHINO. Where - here?

RAISIN. Where I'm at.

CHINO. Up there?...Ahh, yeah - I see you.

RAISIN. I see you.

CHINO. Bye.

RAISIN. No. Come up.

CHINO. To yer crib?

RAISIN. Come upstairs.

CHINO. I don't wanna go upstairs.

RAISIN. Awright - Chino - man?

CHINO. Now?

RAISIN. Come up - Chino, man.

CHINO. Why?

RAISIN. Jus' come up.

CHINO. You come down.

RAISIN. Please - Chino, man.

CHINO. Awright. Don't cry.

RAISIN. *(Paces.)* I ain't crying. You Pendejo. *(He runs to the window again and shouts.)* The door's open.

(CHINO runs in and attempts to push RAISIN out the window. RAISIN screams. CHINO releases RAISIN and laughs.)

RAISIN. Why you gotta play like that - Chino, man.

CHINO. *(laughs)* You got one for me?

RAISIN. One what?

CHINO. Apron. But I want one in baby blue.

RAISIN. Look what you did - Chino, man, you spilled beer on the floor—

CHINO. So?

RAISIN. You spilled beer—

CHINO. Mop it up - you dress for it.

RAISIN. I ain't got a mop.

CHINO. Leave it—

RAISIN. Chino?

CHINO. It's for the dead. *(HE spills a little portion more onto the floor.)*

RAISIN. Stop it - Chino.

CHINO. For all those we know - who ain't here. What do you want home, boy? It's lovely summer day out an' I don't wanna be caged up - I get uptight - fast when I'm locked up. *(HE looks out the window.)* An' La'Jebas are out in full orchestration - Man, I'm so horny the crack of dawn better be careful around me. E'toy culecco. Tu sabe? It's this Puerto Rican blood in me.

RAISIN. Look like you drunk to me, Chino, man.

CHINO. Miller Beer - yeah. Rican blood. You drink, man?

RAISIN. No.

CHINO. Good. Good. Good boy. Good kid. Good fer you. When I was yer age I didn't drink beer. We got good mother's bro. Lemme tell you man...Check it out...The day I drank a beer I got down on a Miller. Shotgun that mother into me - blew me away - been high ever since. *(Shouts out the window.)* Milla. Milla. Milla.

RAISIN. Chino?

CHINO. Raisin.

RAISIN. *(to himself)* Yeah.

CHINO. What?

RAISIN. ...I'm dying.

CHINO. Dying? Where? *(Grabs him.)* Dying here?

RAISIN. I am.

CHINO. D'you know what you talkin' about? 8-foot grave - you know burial. Crying - that kind'ah dying?

RAISIN. I'm dying - Chino.

CHINO. But of what?

RAISIN. I don't know.

CHINO. But you know you dying?

RAISIN. I'm bleeding.

CHINO. Where?

RAISIN. I bled - on the floor - a little while ago.

CHINO. Relax. Lemme think. Lemme look at you. *(long pause)* You ain't dying.

RAISIN. How do you know?

CHINO. I can tell.

RAISIN. Tell me.

CHINO. You can tell when a person is dying.

RAISIN. Tell me - Chino, man...

CHINO. You check out the person's shoulders.

RAISIN. Really - Chino, man?

CHINO. Yeah. Look. The shoulder's turn in like this. You see?

RAISIN. Like that?

CHINO. Like if - you got two great big tit-tees...Two great big fat ones. An' they're too heavy to carry. - You walk around like this...

RAISIN. My tit-tees ain't big.

CHINO. You ain't got none.

RAISIN. No.

CHINO. So - you ain't dying.

RAISIN. No - Chino. It's not my tit-tees. It's my pee-pee.

CHINO. Stay back. Whoa there, Nellie.

RAISIN. Wha - what's wrong?

CHINO. Syphilis - V.D., Jack...Herpies, AIDS, an' all

that kind'ah nasty stuff can kill you.

RAISIN. ...I'm scared, man.

CHINO. Don't bring yer "Plinga" out - I'm scared too.

RAISIN. But I gotta.

CHINO. Why you gotta?

RAISIN. I have to show it to you.

CHINO. Why me?

RAISIN. 'Cause you the oldest guy I know on the block.

CHINO. What about yer ol'man?

RAISIN. I don't got a father. Nobody. But my mother - an' she can't see this.

CHINO. But why do I have to see it? Huh, Bro?

RAISIN. I awready told you.

CHINO. Whatchu pee-pee got to do with you dying?

RAISIN. That's why I wanna show you - Chino, man.

CHINO. You ain't shy - are you?

RAISIN. Awright, Chino, man?

CHINO. I don't know.

RAISIN. Please, Chino, man?

CHINO. Get outta the window. *(RAISIN starts to unzipper his pants.)* Chill. Chill. Take a chill pill for a second - man.

RAISIN. For what?

CHINO. Don't push me - awright? I like doing things my way. Take yer hands outta yer zipper.

RAISIN. But I'm gonna die, Chino.

CHINO. We bury you. So what? *(CHINO paces.)*

RAISIN. Nooo.

CHINO. We all gotta die.

RAISIN. Why live then?

CHINO. So we can die.

RAISIN. Die for what?

CHINO. For nothin'.

RAISIN. Is that true?

CHINO. It's all for nothing.

RAISIN. Nothing?

CHINO. Nada.

RAISIN. What are you looking for?

CHINO. Something.

RAISIN. It's all for nothin'? Huh, Chino? Nada.

CHINO. Yeah. Nothing lives forever - but nothing.

RAISIN. *(depressed)* God.

CHINO. Damn.

RAISIN. And we're nothings. Like the nuns in my school say, "Ashes to ashes - dust to dust."

CHINO. You gotta mask?

RAISIN. A mask for what?

CHINO. To put on.

RAISIN. For me?

CHINO. Nah, for me!

RAISIN. For you to do what?

CHINO. To put on.

RAISIN. For what?

CHINO. I don't wanna breathe in any of yer germs! My hair could fall out, or something.

RAISIN. No. Chino.

CHINO. You ain't got nothin' for my face?

RAISIN. C'mon, Chino. I'm gonna die soon.

CHINO. ...Go 'head. Get yer pee-pee - but do it fast.

The longer I stand here breathing in yer germs - the more risk is involved - there's more of a chance of me contracting something - like dinga-litis. *(CHINO covers his face by putting his arm across it. Crouches down.)*

RAISIN. Awright - Chino?

CHINO. Lift yer apron - I ain't got X-Ray vision. Okay. Be careful you don't get ya pee-pee too close to me. *(RAISIN has lifted his apron. His pants and his underwear HE has removed. And HE is showing his penis to CHINO.)* Lift yer li'l head...Not yer head, man.

RAISIN. You said—

CHINO. Yer head b'tween yer legs! Whatta brain you are - kid.

RAISIN. *(long pause)* See anything?

CHINO. I jus' started. Don't be a back seat driver.

RAISIN. *(long pause)* See anything now?

CHINO. Very interesting.

RAISIN. What - what?!

CHINO. Cover it up quick.

RAISIN. With what?

CHINO. Drop the apron on it. Man - tu ere un Juan Bobo, aren't you?

RAISIN. ...What are you looking for now?

CHINO. Something to cover my hands with.

RAISIN. Like gloves?

CHINO. You got a pair?

RAISIN. For what?

CHINO. I gotta touch yer pee-pee.

RAISIN. For what?

CHINO. I think I know what yer problem is. I jus' wanna make sure. *(Stops looking around the kitchen.)* Forget it. I got something. *(CHINO grabs his beer - removes the brown paper bag it was in and he uses this brown paper bag as a glove - simply by just inserting his hand into it.)* Okay - you ready?

RAISIN. I think. Are you?

CHINO. Wait up. *(HE inhales.)* Let's go.

RAISIN. Is this gonna hurt?

CHINO. I don't know.

RAISIN. *(moves quickly away)* No, Chino, man, forget it.

CHINO. *(exhales)* If it hurts - it's only gonna hurt you a little.

RAISIN. Why only a little?

CHINO. 'Cause you only got a little pee-pee.

RAISIN. Are you sure - Chino, man?

CHINO. Don't worry - yer in good hands with Allstate.

RAISIN. C'mon - Chino?

CHINO. I know what I'm doing.

RAISIN. You done this b'fore?

CHINO. You ain't gonna die.

RAISIN. I'm not gonna die, really?

CHINO. You feeling better awready, right?

RAISIN. Yeah.

CHINO. I told you - I know what I'm doing.

RAISIN. Whatta'ya got to do with me now?

CHINO. I'm gonna take care of business. O.K.? *(CHINO covers his face with his arm and lifts his hand with the brown paper bag. Looking like a surgeon about to operate.)* Let's go - lift the apron. *(RAISIN does. CHINO crouches.)*

RAISIN. *(long pause)* Ooh. Ouch!

CHINO. You know you got blood there.

RAISIN. That's what I been telling you.

CHINO. No problem.

RAISIN. Ouch!

CHINO. Stop moving - Bro.

RAISIN. That bag scratches - Chino.

CHINO. Don't move. I see it - I see it. Uh-ha.

RAISIN. What?

CHINO. Dinga litis.

RAISIN. Oh, God - Chino - What's that?

CHINO. Inflammation of the pee-pee.

RAISIN. Is it serious.

CHINO. Nothing major.

RAISIN. No?

CHINO. Only that...

RAISIN. Only what?

CHINO. Besides having a postage stamp for a dick.

RAISIN. I'm still growing.

CHINO. That's yer problem - well, it's not really a problem. Put yer pants back on. Zip up. Zip up!

RAISIN. *(RAISIN does.)* Am I gonna be all right - Chino?

CHINO. *(Crosses over to the window. Throws the bag he used for a glove out. Sticks his head out the window - inhaling and exhaling loudly.)* Lookit me - man -I'm sweating.

RAISIN. What about me?

CHINO. Nothing.

RAISIN. Nothing's wrong with me?

CHINO. ...What were you doing?

RAISIN. I wasn't doing anything.

CHINO. You gotta cut - on ya pee-pee?

RAISIN. Oh, God, a cut, really? Do I need stitches?

CHINO. It's a little tiny cut.

RAISIN. Man - a cut.

CHINO. You must of been doing something.

RAISIN. Like what?

CHINO. That's what I'm askin' you?

RAISIN. I wasn't doing nothing.

CHINO. C'mon - slick.

RAISIN. Nothing, Chino, man, really.

CHINO. I know you didn't get it shaving.

RAISIN. No.

CHINO. Did you?

RAISIN. No.

CHINO. I didn't see any hairs down - Look'd kind'ah blank.

RAISIN. I'm still growing.

CHINO. True - true. But I can't cure you until I know what you been doing. I don't wanna prescribe the wrong thing by mistake. You still ain't cured - you know.

RAISIN. Do I gotta tell?

CHINO. It's a must. All patients tell their doctors everything.

RAISIN. You ain't gonna tell anybody?

CHINO. Hey, man. We take an oath.

RAISIN. But you're not a doctor.

CHINO. I'm curing you - ain't I?

RAISIN. Uh-huh.

CHINO. I don't need no degree. When it comes to pee-pees - Lookit this shit - Now you got me saying it. When it comes to "pricks." I know all about 'em. I gotta few I know - I'd like to cut off! Serious. Word. Lissin. I got one too - you know?

RAISIN. I know.

CHINO. I've had mine - for way over twenty-five years.

RAISIN. I've had mine for only - since I was born.

CHINO. Which ain't a whole long time. Now, you tell me - who's the man - with the experience here - you or me?

RAISIN. You—

CHINO. Me - right?! Awright then. What was you doing with yer pee-pee? I mean, you know, prick?

RAISIN. ...I was jerking off.

CHINO. You what?!

RAISIN. Yeah.

CHINO. Beating off?

RAISIN. So.

CHINO. *(laughs)* For what? You shoot? You know - something comes outta there? Baya.

RAISIN. C'mon - Chino.

CHINO. La pajita - ha? Lemme shake yer hand - man. Awright. Awright. *(THEY shake hands.)* You sex maniac.

RAISIN. C'mono - Chino.

CHINO. I'm proud of you - you pervert.

RAISIN. C'mon - Chino.

CHINO. You're my kinda - man. Choking the ol' chicken's neck?!! *(CHINO does the gesture of masturbating with his hand.)*

RAISIN. Nijinsky did it.

CHINO. Who - Wha?!

RAISIN. 50 times a day.

CHINO. How many times a day?

RAISIN. 60!

CHINO. This dude choked his bird that many times?

RAISIN. Yep.

CHINO. I'm jealous. That guy is gifted.

RAISIN. That's how he went crazy.

CHINO. Good for 'im. Wasting it like that. Shameful. Shameful thing - bro.

RAISIN. Yeah.

CHINO. Who was this guy?

RAISIN. Nijinsky?

CHINO. Nijinsky - yeah.

RAISIN. My mother—

CHINO. Your mother know this Beyaco?

RAISIN. No.

CHINO. Do I know 'im?

RAISIN. He's dead - Chino.

CHINO. Good! Jerking off like that.

RAISIN. No. Chino. My mother told me he went mad—

CHINO. Crazy - yeah.

RAISIN. From jerking off.

CHINO. Why she tell you something like that?

RAISIN. I don't know.

CHINO. 'Cause she caught you - *(Does the gesture of masturbating with his hand.)* Choking yer chicken.

RAISIN. Yeah.

CHINO. She said it to scare you.

RAISIN. So I won't do it again.

CHINO. I like her. She's a good mother.

RAISIN. Yeah. But she told me he was a great dancer.

CHINO. Not better than me?!

RAISIN. Way better than you.

CHINO. Way better than James Brown?

RAISIN. Nijinsky leaves 'im in the dust.

CHINO. Nah, that's bull. How come I never heard of this guy? Or - how come I never saw him on "Soul Train"?

RAISIN. This is a long time ago, Chino. You know - but my mother says - he was and is the greatest dancer ever live. And she knows - she dancer.

CHINO. She's a go-go dancer.

RAISIN. So?

CHINO. Nobody's better than James Brown.

RAISIN. Okay.

CHINO. Nobody. Or - me. Nobody does the "Elevator Grine" - like I do - the "5000." Or the "Merengue."

RAISIN. No.

CHINO. Awright, then.

RAISIN. But Nijinsky danced ballet. He made 'em up too.

CHINO. Nobody dances ballet. They learn that shit in school. In a class - you gotta go to class for that. What I'm talking about is "Getting Down" groovin'...Cooking, baby, cooking. Serious stuff. Ballet is out. It's out compared to what we do. Ballet - man, is like taking the heart out of a mass murderer and opening it up - you know, cutting it open to see what made it tick - pump - at such a, you know, such a hostile rate. Boring, man. I wanna watch it tick - pump, you know, pump blood hard. Fast. Groovin'. I wanna see it kinda...You know, when it excites itself - The man is jabbing a guy with a knife - it's all - you know...Exciting. Ballet - man. Is the opposite of that - it slows it down. I may not want to see people in slow motion. It may answer a few questions for me - that best stay unanswered. You dig what I'm saying? - Sometimes it's best to stay in the dark. You live happier...I know you don't know what I'm saying. I don't expect you to. I don't expect anybody to. That's why you always see me alone. My kind'ah thinking, it's way above a whole lot of people.

RAISIN. Yeah.

CHINO. A lot of people call it...

RAISIN. Smart.

CHINO. No.

RAISIN. No? Intelligent, then.

CHINO. Nah.

RAISIN. What?

CHINO. Verbal diarrhea. Chino, you talk a lot of shit. They don't care about what I think.

RAISIN. No.

CHINO. They wanna know things like...Why do I always got on long sleeves. Why, when it's 110 degrees out, I got on long sleeves. Maybe I'm a junkie. What am I hiding? That's what they wanna know. Things like that. What's none of their business.

RAISIN. Why do you—

CHINO. Let 'em ask me: What do I think of this "Puta Vida?"

RAISIN. Why do you wear long sleeves?

CHINO. That's none of yer business.

RAISIN. It is hot today - Chino. Gotta be close to ninety.

CHINO. Eighty-nine degrees...Precipitation is expected.

RAISIN. Do you shoot up?

CHINO. I oughtta kick yer ass. Do I shoot up. No.

RAISIN. I'm sorry - Chino, man.

CHINO. I'm into beer, wine, and sex. A lot of sex. I need sex.

RAISIN. How come I never see you around with a girl?

CHINO. 'Cause I don't believe in girlfriends. Dating ain't my cup of tea. I'm into heavy screwing. You like me - you know, we get it on. But don't let me have to feed you first - don't sell yerself that cheaply. That's my way of showin' 'em - I respect them. We fuck - 'cause we wanna fuck. Not 'cause you gotta gimme something - for the Beef Steak Charlies. You know. Then we talk - after we get our rocks off - we introduce each other. Then I be more than happy to cook you a dinner.

RAISIN. I use to think it was because you're real skinny.

CHINO. I ain't that skinny.

RAISIN. You don't think so - Chino?

CHINO. Skinny to me is flesh and bones - skinny.

RAISIN. Yeah.

CHINO. I'm lean.

RAISIN. I never see you wear shorts.

CHINO. I don't like shorts.

RAISIN. Every time - everybody gets together to go to the beach you never go.

CHINO. Yeah.

RAISIN. You don't like gettin' sun?

CHINO. I love the sun.

RAISIN. How 'bout the water?

CHINO. I love the water.

RAISIN. You never go to the pool.

CHINO. How do you know all this? You been watching me.

RAISIN. No.

CHINO. For what?

RAISIN. I jus' see you all by yerself all the time.

CHINO. I told you why.

RAISIN. When everybody on the block goes to Bear Mountain, you know, the block is deserted. There's nobody on the block but you.

CHINO. Yeah.

RAISIN. I don't know?

CHINO. What do you want me to say?

RAISIN. I don't know.

CHINO. You feel sorry for me?

RAISIN. ...Yeah.

CHINO. Oh, yeah? Why, 'cause I'm a swizzle-stick?

RAISIN. No.

CHINO. Why then?

RAISIN. 'Cause I like you. *(awkward silence)*

CHINO. You like me.

RAISIN. You're a nice guy.

CHINO. I'm a nice guy.

RAISIN. And you're always around.

CHINO. *(Long uncomfortable pause.)* I like you.

RAISIN. You do - Chino?

CHINO. Yeah.

RAISIN. I know.

CHINO. I feel sorry for you sometimes - you're always

locked up here—

RAISIN. I know.

CHINO. I always catch you looking out yer window.

RAISIN. I know.

CHINO. Your mother don't like you going out?

RAISIN. No.

CHINO. How come she don't let you go downstairs? Don't let you sit on the stoop for a little while?

RAISIN. She don't, that's all.

CHINO. An' yer Pops? I never saw yer Pops.

RAISIN. I never saw my Pops either.

CHINO. Do you care?

RAISIN. No.

CHINO. If you were to see 'im?

RAISIN. Nothing.

CHINO. 'Cause you don't care.

RAISIN. Yeah.

CHINO. They told me your father was black?

RAISIN. He was mixed.

CHINO. Your mother digs black guys?

RAISIN. He was mixed.

CHINO. Your mother is a fine Latina - lemme tell you. Yeah. Sometimes I can't look at her, that's how fine she is. *(long pause)* You fine too.

RAISIN. ...Thanks.

CHINO. *(long pause)* Who gave you that name - Raisin?

RAISIN. ...I think it was my father.

CHINO. Why?

RAISIN. 'Cause when I was born - I came out dark - like a raisin.

CHINO. But you ain't that dark.

RAISIN. I changed color as I got older. I got lighter.

CHINO. I dig. That's like some people, you know like the white people. When they were kids - you know, they were born with blond hair. When they got older - their hair changed color - it got darker. I used to have blond hair.

RAISIN. Really?

CHINO. Bullshit! I hate when Ricans say that shit. *(Uses a female voice.)* Oh, yeah, man. I used to have blond hair. *(Back to his own natural voice.)* They get off on that shit, you know? That they once coulda gotten over. Yeah. As far over as the black woman with the blond wig did! Right! *(HE laughs to himself.)* What - would you rather be?

RAISIN. I don't understand - Chino - Be what?

CHINO. ...Be.

RAISIN. Yeah.

CHINO. Be.

RAISIN. Be like?

CHINO. Be most. Do you like yer Combo. Black - Latino?

RAISIN. I don't think about it. I do sometimes...get embarrassed.

CHINO. Embarrassed...Like what? Tell me.

RAISIN. When I get into a fight - like say with a black kid.

CHINO. Uh-huh.

RAISIN. And I get so mad - I want to say to 'im - you know - "You Nigger!" A lot of times I think of my father and myself. And I...I jus' shut up. But sometimes I say it. But I feel bad afterwards.

CHINO. Say it.

RAISIN. For what?

CHINO. C'mon.

RAISIN. No.

CHINO. Nigguh.

RAISIN. *(long pause)* Yeah. So?

CHINO. How you feel?

RAISIN. I feel - mad - 'cause you said it to me.

CHINO. But if you was to say it to somebody else—

RAISIN. I wouldn't feel bad - 'cause I'm not talkin' about me.

CHINO. *(smiles)* You lil' nigguh.

RAISIN. Stoppit - Chino.

CHINO. I'm only playing wit' ya, man.

RAISIN. I know. I jus' get mixed up.

CHINO. Well - I think it's nice. It'll be hard to take sides without you feelin' it. You know?...In this black and white world.

RAISIN. I don't know - I don't understand - sometimes.

CHINO. *(long pause)* Why don't you sit on my lap?

RAISIN. Sit on ya lap?

CHINO. Sit on my lap - yeah.

RAISIN. I don't understand.

CHINO. Sit on my lap.

RAISIN. But I'm not a - *(He wants to say "girl".)*

CHINO. Sit on my lap.

RAISIN. ...I'm not a girl.

CHINO. I know you're not a girl.

RAISIN. Why should I sit on your lap?

CHINO. 'Cause I came up here.

RAISIN. I know.

CHINO. You sit on my lap - an' I'll tell you a poem.

RAISIN. What poem?

CHINO. A peom I wrote.

RAISIN. You wrote a poem?

CHINO. You don't believe I wrote a poem?

RAISIN. You probably copied if offa somebody.

CHINO. Nah, man, I don't do that. I got my own empty head - an' I keep it that way. But I got talent - man - you don't know.

RAISIN. What's the poem about?

CHINO. You gonna sit on my lap?

RAISIN. *(long pause)* You really wrote a poem? *(CHINO nods "yes".)* Lemme see it.

CHINO. It's in my head.

RAISIN. Memorized.

CHINO. I got it memorized.

RAISIN. Is it a nice poem?

CHINO. You're gonna like it - man - I guarantee it. *(A long pause. RAISIN moves toward Chino - Separates his legs and sits on his lap.)*

RAISIN. Am I too heavy?

CHINO. Nah.

RAISIN. O.K. Lemme hear - *(looks at Chino)* Let's hear your poem. *(CHINO smiles. RAISIN starts to get up.)* I knew you didn't have no poem.

CHINO. *(Holds him down.)* No - no - I got it.

RAISIN. Well, c'mon - Chino, man?

CHINO. *(Long pause. Fiercely blurts out:)*

Blazing! *(RAISIN is startled.)*

Blazing in rust. My abandon building seemed to stare sullenly

Erected. Hardened.
Like
The bulge in a child molester's pants!
The building's spirit induced us kids to surrender.
(Gently, quietly, HE says:)
Come here. Look what I got for you. I got a candy
    cane.
—It seem to say. And the game of leap-frog was
    played.

The abandon building stooped down
Like the child molester
—and allowed us to vault over its table and chairs
Getting a kick every time one of us kids landed on it har-
    dened floor. Flat on our ass.

Now at the feet of Mercy
Laying his face out for anyone to smack - the Building—
Like
the freckle-faced kid with the protruding tooth—
Gets its windows punched out by the bulldozer.

Wait!

The Foreman (Judge and Jury)
Condescended to grant an audience to the friends of the
    condemned building.

We kids went in for the last time and had ourselves one
    hell of a
time with this building.

touching this and feeling that.

It was a slam-bang
thank you sir good time.

Kissing his bonnet to the wind
the building went
Crumbling...
That's it. You like it?

RAISIN. *(long pause)* I'm not stupid - Chino...I'm not stupid.

CHINO. *(Trying to keep RAISIN from noticing his intentions.)* Me too. I'm not stupid either. So?

RAISIN. I know you're not.

CHINO. *(toying)* Don't forget it.

RAISIN. I know what you're doing - Chino. I'm not afraid of you.

CHINO. What am I doing - Wha?

RAISIN. I'm not afraid of you.

CHINO. *(getting upset)* I know. O.K.

RAISIN. *(to himself)* I'm not afraid of you.

CHINO. *(pretending)* No?

RAISIN. You like what you're doing - I know.

CHINO. Oh, yeah?

RAISIN. I know you do.

CHINO. An' whatta 'bout you?

RAISIN. I'm not afraid of you.

CHINO. *(soothingly)* What's there to be afraid of?

RAISIN. You know.

CHINO. *(Looks at Raisin with meaning.)* You think that's why I asked you to sit on my lap?

RAISIN. You like me.

CHINO. I like you - yeah.

RAISIN. You like men?

CHINO. Not me.

RAISIN. What am I?

CHINO. You're a boy. *(RAISIN, who has listened vigorously now, stops to think what has been said. Edging forward - to get up - he accidentally touches Chino's groin.)*

RAISIN. *(Immediately, angrily, HE springs to his feet.)* Shit - Chino - man. You gotta boner.

CHINO. *(Defensively, giving himself away. Swiftly.)* It's an accident - Raisin, man. An accident. *(Grabs Raisin close.)*

RAISIN. Let go—

CHINO. *(bear-hugs Raisin)* I'm only playing with you - man. *(RAISIN struggles half-heartedly. Bends forward. Chino, still holding him, will close his eyes enjoying Raisin. HE will laugh - pressing himself against Raisin.)*

RAISIN. Stoppit, Chino.

CHINO. *(beseechingly)* Why can't I play with you? - I'm only playing with you. *(CHINO'S eyes remain shut.)*

RAISIN. Not like this, Chino. *(Awkward silence. RAISIN stops struggling. Still quietly, Chino releases Raisin.)*

CHINO. I gotta go.

RAISIN. Yeah. *(HE is upset.)*

CHINO. Lissen - about yer pee-pee.

RAISIN. *(tightly)* Forget it. *(Walks over to the window - stares our.)*

CHINO. Lemme tell you. *(Almost pleading with Raisin.)*

RAISIN. No.

CHINO. *(intently)* Lemme tell you something—

RAISIN. *(having had enough)* No - awright?!

CHINO. No.

RAISIN. *(tentatively)* I know what you are.

CHINO. *(matter-of-factly)* The devil.

RAISIN. No.

CHINO. *(bitterly)* I'm the devil.

RAISIN. *(Pause. Almost plaintively - as a child would be.)* You're the devil.

CHINO. *(Waits a long time, and then in a new mood.)* No! I'm a horny dude, that's all. Yeah. *(RAISIN is silent and sullen.)* I'd fuck anything on two legs.

RAISIN. *(Trying to recover from the shock.)* You mean ...anything - Chino - really?

CHINO. *(Pause. Knows he should not have spoken so quickly.)* Well, you know...almost anything.

RAISIN. A man is one of 'em.

CHINO. *(More frustrated than annoyed that he has to explain to Raisin his sexuality.)* No!

RAISIN. *(encouraged)* But when I sat on your lap - Chino - you got a boner.

CHINO. 'Cause yer ass was on it!

RAISIN. But I'm not a girl.

CHINO. You got an ass—

RAISIN. Yeah.

CHINO. Awright then?

RAISIN. That's wrong - ain't it - Chino?

RAISIN. Don't you feel—

CHINO. I feel nothing - man. I know what I'm doing.

RAISIN. But we're not suppose to.

CHINO. Who? Who's not suppose to?

RAISIN. Us.

CHINO. Us home boys from around here?

RAISIN. You and me.

CHINO. What you and me? No, you and me. Me! Jus'
me - man. You're always locked up here in the house.
What do you know about this "Puta Vida?" Huh?
...Nothin'. Except maybe what you've seen from ya window. I'm down on the street all the time. You seen
me, right?

RAISIN. I know. Yeah.

CHINO. It goes with the territory. That's all I can
say.

RAISIN. I don't understand - Chino.

CHINO. There's nothin' to understand. You said - us,
right? That was what you said.

RAISIN. Yeah.

CHINO. Awright then. You said - us.

RAISIN. So.

CHINO. Meaning—

RAISIN. You and me.

CHINO. No!

RAISIN. No - okay.

CHINO. Meaning: Us street-fighting men. That...us
street fighting men...ain't suppose to be into weird things
like that.

RAISIN. No, you're not.

CHINO. Yeah, O.K....We're suppose to be into what
every street dude has been into since the collar was inven-
ted and some cat - probably by the name of Rocky an' shit
came along and turned it up - Dracula style - to show guys
like us are only one thing - Street Fighting Men Out

for Blood.

RAISIN. No - Chino.

CHINO. Yeah. Then we learn how to cuff our wrists - ape style.

RAISIN. Nooo.

CHINO. Yeah. We even began to take on the shape of an ape. You seen how we walk down the street. *(does it)* No wonder people say we belong in a cage.

RAISIN. No, c'mon, Chino.

CHINO. Yeah. Lissen - I'll give you that much. We're all li'l fucking - monkeys.

RAISIN. I didn't say that.

CHINO. Playing and screwing with each other.

RAISIN. No - Chino.

CHINO. Yeah. I'm the first to admit it. But who died and left me Tarzan over us Apes?

RAISIN. Huh - Chino?

CHINO. ...You're right. I am skinny. Being skinny - ugly skinny - has given me a lot of time alone. Time that if I looked like everybody else - I'd be doing the things everybody else does. Having a good time. You know - how I explain - "My Thing." You know?

RAISIN. No.

CHINO. No - you don't know? Or, no - you don't know what I'm talking about?!

RAISIN. No - I don't know what you're talking about.

CHINO. You know what I did.

RAISIN. ...Yeah.

CHINO. You know—

RAISIN. No.

CHINO. C'mon, man, when I told you to sit on my lap.

RAISIN. Oh, yeah, that.

CHINO. That's good you're awready forgetting. One thing you gotta know.

RAISIN. *(long pause)* Yeah?

CHINO. *(long pause)* I don't receive. I deliver...Like a true street fighting man. I give it to the guy - I don't go down on nobody. I'm the man. Sex is sex - anyway you put it - it's an X-clamation point! *(CHINO stands grandly, feeling good having gotten it out of his system and having heard himself out loud. HE feels what he has said does make sense after all. It's a "Puta Life" anyway. Raisin is gaining confidence in his friend Chino because of the interest in his face. Chino faces him to talk to Raisin.)* Now...what's happening with yer pee-pee is...nothing. Nothing at all. You jus' haven't been circumcised. No big deal.

RAISIN. You sure, Chino?

CHINO. Jus' don't pull on it hard. 'Cause when you pull back you're stretching that little piece of skin that's attached under yer cock to yer foreskin. Want me to show you? Pull yer thing out.

RAISIN. No, no. That's awright, Chino.

CHINO. *(laughs)* The cut you got - awright - is what's causing the bleeding. That'll heal. Next time - *(CHINO is getting ready to exit.)* - you jerk off.

RAISIN. Nah, I ain't gonna jerk-off no more.

CHINO. Yeah, right! Jus' don't get aggressive on yourself. Take it light - treat it gently. You take it easy. Do - you do like the guy who works the elevator in my factory. He always says, "Chino, take it easy. Inch by inch the elephant fucked the ant!" You ever nail a chick...or whatever...you'll know what he's talking about. Serious - words to live by!

(CHINO exits. RAISIN crosses over to the window - looks out. The sounds of the CONGA increase - and climax to an end.)

BLACKOUT

POPPA DIO!

CHARACTERS

ANGELO: *Mid-thirties. Hispanic. Is tall, restless and commanding. Angelo is a man consumed with that drive to have it all. Happiness, money, women.*

MAFIA: *Is her stage name—from when she was performing in Boston's "Combat Zone" as a stripper. She is the mother of Angelo, and she is fifty years old. But she looks as old as her son, somewhere between her late thirties and early forties. Young, eager, well-built. Clearly a woman from the backwoods of Puerto Rico. Still eager, desirous, even anxious—keenly in search of life and for love. Trembling on the brink of despair. Also not afraid to take the final leap.*

SCENE: Angelo and Mafia's kitchen in the South Bronx. Basically, it is a kitchen similar to the one in "NIJINSKY CHOKED HIS CHICKEN." The only difference is that Angelo and Mafia's kitchen is littered with garbage, beer bottles and clothes. The major difference is that this particular family possesses a telephone! The lights in this kitchen are dimmed— to 15 watts. A typical and undistinguished unhappy home.

TIME: Autumn.

SCENE 1

AT RISE: Midnight. All LIGHTS are down but the corner STREETLAMP, shining through the window lighting the stage dimly. The faint sounds of a WOMAN CRYING are heard and increase in volume. It is more in anguish than hysteria. The audience will only see her bare legs. MAFIA is in her nightgown, laying on the floor where she had fallen from being struck.

ANGELO. *(In a fury. HE enters the stage, looking around the kitchen.)* I hate you! God, I hate you! I hate you so fuckin' much! *(Crosses over to the refrigerator, looks to the side of it and takes out a baseball bat. ANGELO silently stands, holding the baseball bat, glaring down on Mafia. MAFIA wakes instantly, perceives his action, and crawls over to Angelo.)*

MAFIA. *(Sobs.)* No, no, no, no. *(ANGELO raises the baseball bat over his head. MAFIA sobs uncontrollably.)* No, no, no, no!

(MAFIA turns away, too weak to stand and run. SHE crawls, rushing toward the exit. ANGELO pursues her. Silently. Calmly. When SHE has exited, ANGELO will stop at the edge of the exit, raise his hand, and proceed to beat Mafia with it. Taking sharp, precise, shots at her. The audience is only seeing ANGELO lift and come down with the bat. They will also be hearing the thud and her GROANS. ANGELO will swing the bat until he is exhausted, building his swing until the bat falls from his grasp.)

ANGELO. *(Turns and faces the audience, eyes full of tears.)*

76

Poppa Dio!... *(Drops to his knees.)* Poppa Dio... *(Sobs.)* I beat
her to death. *(Covers his face with his hands, sobbing uncontrollably. "Poppa Dio," he repeats over and over.)* I beat her to
death ... My mother ... Poppa Dio! I killed her, Poppa
Dio! ... I killed my mother. *(Sobs, and covers his face again.)*
Poppa Dio! Poppa Dio!... *(LIGHTS slowly dim out.)*

SCENE 2

TIME: A few hours earlier.

*AT RISE. The RADIO on top of the refrigerator is going.
ANGELO stands at the window looking down at the street
below. HE is dressed soberly in a dark suit, shirt and tie. Is
smoking a cigarette. Presently, MAFIA is by the stove stirring a pot of rice with a large cooking spoon. SHE is in her
nightgown, and is barefooted. MAFIA looks over at her son
in fascination. ANGELO loudly snorts—three times.*

MAFIA. Spit that out.
ANGELO. *(Without looking over at her.)* Too late. I
swallowed it.
MAFIA. ... It turns my stomach.
ANGELO. It coats mine. *(SHE gives up on him and starts to
stir the pot of rice again. ANGELO listens to the music, with his
eyes far away— MAFIA is dumbfounded. SHE purposely slams
her cooking spoon against her pot of rice.)* What was that?
The phone?

MAFIA. No!

(The TELEPHONE rings.)

ANGELO. That's for me. *(MAFIA turns off the RADIO. It is obvious that SHE wants to listen.)* Why you turn off the radio? *(HE answers the telephone.)* Hello? Yeah, this is Angelo. What's wrong? *(MAFIA looks at her son, not stirring the rice. A long silence.)* Why you doin' this? What did I do wrong?!

MAFIA. Who's that - Virgin?

ANGELO. *(Pauses heavily. Depressed. Deeply hurt.)* That's not a reason.

MAFIA. It's Virgin - I know it's Virgin.

ANGELO. I wanna see you.

MAFIA. Hang up - hang up on her.

ANGELO. Please, Virgin.

MAFIA. *(angry)* Gimme the phone. *(Reaches out for it.)*

ANGELO. *(Turns on her.)* What are you doing?!!!!

MAFIA. Gimme the phone.

ANGELO. I'm on the phone.

MAFIA. It's my phone.

ANGELO. I wanna see you, Virgin.

MAFIA. *(angry)* E'tupido.

ANGELO. *(Gives her a hard stare.)* You at yer mother's?

MAFIA. That phone is mine - I pay for it.

ANGELO. She called me!

MAFIA. So what?

ANGELO. Here. Here, here. *(HE goes into his pocket - counts off a few dollars - and throws them on the floor at his mother's feet.)*

MAFIA. *(Furious - kicks the money.)* E'tupido. Animal!

ANGELO. Come over, Virgin.

MAFIA. I don't want that slut here. *(ANGELO punches the wall.)*

MAFIA. Good. That's good. Bang your face! Go 'head. Better.

ANGELO. Don't leave me, Virgin.

MAFIA. *(laughs)* Ha! I told you.

ANGELO. Don't go to Puerto Rico. Lemme talk to you.

MAFIA. Oh - I thank God.

ANGELO. I love you, Virgin.

MAFIA. *(furious)* Que 'stupido!

ANGELO. Virgin?...Virgin? Hello, Virgin?

MAFIA. Hang up - she's gone.

ANGELO. *(About to break down.)* Virgin?

MAFIA. *(SHE roughly snatches the phone from him.)* Hang up.

ANGELO. *(HE snatches back the phone.)* Virgin? *(HE is quietly sobbing. The words pour out with urgency and desperation.)* Virgin? I'm not feeling good...*(MAFIA gestures with bitter disgust.)* I know you're still there - I love you, Virgin - Come over, Virgin? Come over. *(HE sobs.)*

MAFIA. *(Snatches the phone and hangs it up.)* You got no shame. It turns my stomach. *(SHE walks over to her stove - stirs her pot of rice. ANGELO walks over to the window and loudly sobs.)* Go to bed. Lay down. *(SHE loudly strikes her spoon against the pot of rice.)*

ANGELO. Stop that! Stoppit! *(HE sobs. Opens the window.)*

MAFIA. Why are you opening the window? Don't open

the window - it's cold outside. *(ANGELO sobs, pacing.)* Close the window.

ANGELO. *(Lunges for the window with a loud sigh. MAFIA screams!)* I wanna die!

MAFIA. *(Leaps forward and wraps her arms tightly around his waist. ANGELO sobs on the window sill. SHE is angered.)* Come inside. C'mon. You want people to see you?

ANGELO. I don't care. *(Loudly sighs. MAFIA leaves him at the window. Walks over to her stove. Stirs her pot of rice. Long silence. SHE loudly strikes the pot with her cooking spoon.)* Stoppit! Stop that.

MAFIA. Close the window. *(Long pause. Strikes the pot again loudly.)*

ANGELO. Okay. Okay. *(HE closes the window.)*

MAFIA. Siddown - eat something.

ANGELO. *(Sits. To himself.)* I want her.

MAFIA. What did you say?

ANGELO. Nothing. *(HE stands and walks over to the phone.)*

MAFIA. You're not gonna call her. *(Slams her pot loudly.)* You better not call her.

ANGELO. I want to.

MAFIA. *(While serving him, filling his plate with rice and beans.)* Not on my phone.

ANGELO. *(angry)* Why not?!

MAFIA. *(disgusted)* 'Cause this...this...bitch - don't love you!

ANGELO. Her name is Virgin.

MAFIA. Bitch.

ANGELO. Virgin.

MAFIA. Bitch. She don't love you.

ANGELO. That ain't true.

MAFIA. Bitch! *(Slams her pot.)* It's true.

ANGELO. *(Walks over to her, snatches the cooking spoon away from her, and repeatedly bangs the pot of rice with it.)* Ha? Ha?! *(HE stops.)* Okay?

MAFIA. Animal. *(Slams the plate of rice and beans on the table. ANGELO snorts loudly.)* Spit that out. *(ANGELO sits down to eat.)* She only loved you when you had money.

ANGELO. *(Lifts the fork.)* I'm eating. Awright?

MAFIA. *(Everytime ANGELO attempts to eat, MAFIA will interrupt hime - by speaking. At which time HE simply lowers his fork and stares out into space.)* When you were shot in Brooklyn—

ANGELO. Not again - Don't bring that up again.

MAFIA. When you were shot at the bar in Brooklyn.

ANGELO. I'm eating.

MAFIA. They told me she was there with you.

ANGELO. *(Drops the fork on his plate loudly.)* Who told you that, huh? Who the frig' told you that?! Who?

MAFIA. Somebody.

ANGELO. Who - somebody?! *(ANGELO lifts his fork.)*

MAFIA. They told me - she ran - out into the street - with all the other people who were at the bar.

ANGELO. *(angry)* That's a lie. Who told you all this?

MAFIA. They told me the bartender dragged you outta the bar—

ANGELO. That's about the only thing you said that's true.

MAFIA. And he locked the bar and left you on the street to die.

ANGELO. Yeah. So?

MAFIA. *(angry)* Where was this bitch?

ANGELO. *(angry)* I don't know, awright?! Lemme eat! *(ANGELO attempts to put the fork in his mouth.)*

MAFIA. You're an old man. *(ANGELO loudly drops the fork on his plate.)* What she gonna do with an old man?

ANGELO. Lemme eat!

MAFIA. She's a twenty-year-old girl. You went - like a fool - you went out - and spent all this...this...money you made - I don't know how - I don't wanna know. I just know you - like a fool - spent it all on her.

ANGELO. I made it bartending.

MAFIA. Bartending? Bartending, my beautiful fat ass. You was a barfly maybe, but not a bartender. She took your money.

ANGELO. Nobody takes my money. I'm not a Puta.

MAFIA. Ha!!

ANGELO. I'm a Puta?!

MAFIA. You bought her a car.

ANGELO. I bought her a car - yeah.

MAFIA. 'Cause she wanted it.

ANGELO. 'Cause I wanted too.

MAFIA. 'Cause she wanted it.

ANGELO. Lemme eat - please.

MAFIA. What did you buy me?

ANGELO. These rice and beans. I'd like to eat 'em.

MAFIA. Ralphie.

ANGELO. *(Nasty. Mimics MAFIA.)* May he rest in peace.

MAFIA. May he rest in peace. Yeah, that's right. May he rest in peace.

ANGELO. *(angry)* Okay.

MAFIA. He was your best friend.

ANGELO. He was my only friend.

MAFIA. I remember. May he rest in peace. I remember the day he told me - you could—

ANGELO. I know - I could—

MAFIA. Yeah. You could have—

ANGELO and MAFIA. *(together)* Bought a house!

MAFIA. Bought me a house, that's right.

ANGELO. *(upset)* With what?

MAFIA. With what?!

ANGELO. All I want to do is eat and go, awright? I didn't come here to argue.

MAFIA. What happened to all the money you had?

ANGELO. What money I had?

MAFIA. Ralphie told me you had thousands.

ANGELO. Oh, yeah, I had millions - not thousands - millions!

MAFIA. That's right.

ANGELO. Get outta here. I didn't have that much.

MAFIA. Enough for a down-payment on a house.

ANGELO. Okay, I did. Awright - lemme eat something.

MAFIA. Enough to send Esa Pendeja - that four-legged garbage pickin' cat - to Spain.

ANGELO. You know - you're beautiful.

MAFIA. I'm fuckin' mad.

ANGELO. Not with my food - okay?

MAFIA. What did she do to get all this money outta you? Did she rub a piece of steak between her legs and feed it to you?

ANGELO. Rub what?

MAFIA. If a woman wants to tame a man - have him by his pride - his nuts—

ANGELO. I know where his pride is.

MAFIA. All she has to do before she cooks 'im his steak is rub it on her pussy.

ANGELO. And that'll tame 'm? *(HE laughs.)*

MAFIA. How many steaks did she feed you?

ANGELO. *(ANGELO is still laughing.)* Nah - I just ate her - no steaks. Why you always wait till I sit down to argue with me?

MAFIA. It's the only time - you won't walk out on me. Leave me with my words in my mouth.

ANGELO. Can I eat? I'd like to put something in my mouth.

MAFIA. Here, lemme cook you a steak.

ANGELO. That's awright. *(A long silence as HE finally gets an opportunity to eat. MAFIA looks at him. HE stops.)* Don't look at me, okay? I don't like to be looked at when I'm eating.

MAFIA. A hora se yo? I'm not looking at you.

ANGELO. No, that's right, I was looking at you.

MAFIA. Yeah, you were lookin' at me!

ANGELO. I'm sorry - my mistake.

MAFIA. So delicate. *(A long silence.)*

ANGELO. No!

MAFIA. I know.

ANGELO. Huh?

MAFIA. I know you ain't delicate. I carried you inside here - *(Smacks her stomach loudly.)* Nine months - you scratching and kicking every day of those months -like a brute.

ANGELO. I am a brute.

MAFIA. I didn't say you were a brute.

ANGELO. I am.

MAFIA. You ain't delicate.

ANGELO. I ain't delicate, awright. You're the boss and I'm the hoss.

MAFIA. I gave you life.

ANGELO. Yeah. You're the boss and I'm the hoss. Now, you mind if I put on the feedbag?

MAFIA. I mind seeing you going around borrowing money to pay for her car.

ANGELO. What's that got to do with you?

MAFIA. Everything.

ANGELO. Am I taking food outta yer mouth?!

MAFIA. It has everything to do with me.

ANGELO. Do you see me taking food outta yer mouth??

MAFIA. *(furious)* What the hell have you given me?

ANGELO. Am I taking food outta yer mouth?

MAFIA. A house?!

ANGELO. You can't eat a house.

MAFIA. *(Slams her hand down on the kitchen table loudly.)* I want to live in one.

ANGELO. Go 'head - who's stoppin' you?

MAFIA. *(Suddenly, with hate and agony, screaming.)* YOU! *(SHE throws his plate of food onto the floor.)*

ANGELO. *(not disturbed)* That was nice. Why don't you throw the whole pot of rice on the floor? *(MAFIA does.)* It's only money. I can always buy a bag of potato chips.

MAFIA. Eat on the floor, you animal - only an animal treats his mother the way you do.

ANGELO. I treat you bad?

MAFIA. YES!

ANGELO. Whatta I do? Do I throw yer food on the floor like you always do to me?

MAFIA. *(in anguish)* You've left me here...in this place.

ANGELO. What do you want me to do? Go out and hold up people?

MAFIA. Yes.

ANGELO. You do?!

MAFIA. Yes.

ANGELO. Awright. *(HE stands up to leave.)* How many people you want me to rob?

MAFIA. ...As many as I had to go to bed with! *(There is total silence. ANGELO looks at his mother without recognition.)* You stand there - actin' like you didn't know? Innocent!

ANGELO. *(Not wanting to believe her.)* You mean...You were a 'ho?

MAFIA. *(Accusing him.)* Guilty!

ANGELO. ...You mean...I'm guilty? Guilty of what?!

MAFIA. Of being innocent.

ANGELO. *(In sudden anger, frightened agony. Turning madly.)* ...Don't do it...please don't do it...Man, not with me. *(furious)* I'm not gonna let you do it.

MAFIA. *(Slowly, maliciously. Slowly for effect.)* Like violin notes on blue marble, I landed on the beds of cops, doctors, and lawyers, and creeps. But I ain't tellin' you nothin' you didn't know.

ANGELO. I was a kid.

MAFIA. Innocent.

ANGELO. Innocent - yeah.

MAFIA. But you had eyes—

ANGELO. Innocence.

MAFIA. You were blind?

ANGELO. Innocent.

MAFIA. Blind to what was going on.

ANGELO. I saw.

MAFIA. And you didn't care.

ANGELO. You were my mother. How could I really believe my eyes.

MAFIA. I watched you - I watched you - watch me. Think.

ANGELO. No.

MAFIA. Think back.

ANGELO. No. I was a kid.

MAFIA. Innocent.

ANGELO. Yeah.

MAFIA. Guilty.

ANGELO. Why am I guilty?

MAFIA. 'Cause you didn't stay innocent.

ANGELO. *(adamantly)* You're not gonna drive me crazy.

MAFIA. Not for long. You didn't stay innocent - for long. *(advances)* You continued to watch me. You wanted food - so you watched me. You wanted a bed to sleep in. So you watched me. You wanted clothes - so you watched me. You wanted money - so you took it from me. *(SHE takes on a sensuous mood. Takes his face in her hands and passionately kisses her son on the lips.)* My pimp. *(long pause)* Remember how I used to always kiss you on the lips?

ANGELO. Remember how I never liked it.

MAFIA. ...I haven't kissed you—

ANGELO. In a long time.

MAFIA. Years.

ANGELO. Don't ever kiss me like that again. I swear, don't. *(long pause)*

MAFIA. I can do anything I want - I carried you nine months in pain. I gotta right to enjoy the fruit of my labor.

ANGELO. That's what you call enjoying?

MAFIA. What did you call it when you came down to the club and watched me dance...Naked...in front of all those men?

ANGELO. Nothing.

MAFIA. I saw your eyes - felt 'em all over me. Beckoning - felt 'em beckoning me to hurry and take it all off.

ANGELO. No - that's wrong.

MAFIA. No - you wasn't innocent. Over twenty-one, an' a man.

ANGELO. You were a pro. You raised me to always think you were a professional. You never took your job home.

MAFIA. That's right.

ANGELO. I came down to the club - jus' to come down.

MAFIA. I was a professional.

ANGELO. Yeah.

MAFIA. Mafia - they called me down in the "Combat Zone" when I worked in Boston. Mafia. Presenting Mafia! I was big. I was powerful. Mafia! You watched me.

ANGELO. Yeah - I watched you.

MAFIA. I love you.

ANGELO. I hate you.

MAFIA. *(Looking at him.)* Mafia!

ANGELO. ...for making it all so damn casual. Natural. I thought it was natural for me to go and see you. Since I was a kid—

MAFIA. Innocent.

ANGELO. No.

MAFIA. You watched me.

ANGELO. I watched you...From one strip joint to another. From Boston to Baltimore.

MAFIA. You watched me.

ANGELO. I watched you.

MAFIA. I hate you.

ANGELO. I love you. I watched you.

MAFIA. *(shouts)* Mafia!

ANGELO. I hate myself.

MAFIA. I love you.

ANGELO. I hate myself.

MAFIA. I love you.

ANGELO. I hate myself.

MAFIA. Watch me. *(SHE throws her arms up above her head and slowly comes down feeling her breasts, hip and thighs.)*

ANGELO. I remember... *(MAFIA continues to repeat the action of caressing herself.)* One time, I dropped by - when you were working at the Pink Pussy Cat. We were living in Boston. That night you wasn't dancing. You were - just working for the car - commission.

MAFIA. I was hustling for drinks.

ANGELO. *(Gives her a hard stare for a long moment.)* I was

around twenty-two—

MAFIA. *(SHE stops caressing and begins to slowly dance.)* I wanted you to take care of me.

ANGELO. I know.

MAFIA. You work and I take care of the house.

ANGELO. I know, ma.

MAFIA. I cook for you.

ANGELO. I sat down next to you - you were sitting next to this old guy.

MAFIA. I remember - I kissed you.

ANGELO. Yeah.

MAFIA. On the lips.

ANGELO. *(upset)* Yeah. You told the guy I was yer boyfriend.

MAFIA. —how could I tell 'im you was my son? What kinda son would let his mother work in a place like that? *(stops dancing)* Without feeling ashamed for his mother, or himself!

ANGELO. I hate you...for raising me to feel no shame.

MAFIA. I love you.

ANGELO. The worst was when you told me one time to buy yer boss a drink. I was 18 years old - and you were working down on the block in Baltimore. I didn't have a job. I was outta school and didn't have any money to buy 'im a drink.

MAFIA. I know. I asked the man sitting next to me to gimme five dollars.

ANGELO. And you kissed him.

MAFIA. I love you.

ANGELO. I turned my head - made believe I didn't see you.

MAFIA. I watched you.

ANGELO. You gave me the five and I bought yer boss a drink with it. I hate you. I felt no shame. *(Their feelings hang in the room. MAFIA stares out into space. ANGELO stares out the window.)*

MAFIA. I don't like you.

ANGELO. I know.

MAFIA. *(very quietly)* You know.

ANGELO. I did nothing.

MAFIA. I've done everything for you.

ANGELO. You did.

MAFIA. I still do everything for you.

ANGELO. ...You do.

MAFIA. I don't like you.

ANGELO. I know.

MAFIA. No more.

ANGELO. O.K. I won't come around.

MAFIA. You need a bed to sleep—

ANGELO. I know.

MAFIA. The door is always—

ANGELO. I know.

MAFIA. It's always open.

ANGELO. O.K.

MAFIA. Awright?

ANGELO. It's O.K.

MAFIA. I can't rely on you.

ANGELO. No.

MAFIA. I can't see you—

ANGELO. No.

MAFIA. Not doing anything for me.

ANGELO. No. *(A heavy silence. ANGELO crosses, moving*

towards the exit. Quiet. MAFIA, without looking up at him, crosses over to the window.)

MAFIA. ...I pass this window every evening.

ANGELO. Lemme give 'ya a few bucks.

MAFIA. I gotta few bucks on the floor.

ANGELO. That...I was mad. *(Bends down to pick up the three dollars he threw on the floor when he was on the phone.)*

MAFIA. Leave it.

ANGELO. *(annoyed)* What?

MAFIA. I pass this window every evening.

ANGELO. What - what are you saying?

MAFIA. During my "Happy Hour."

ANGELO. Happy Hour?

MAFIA. I have a Happy Hour. An hour where I stand here in front of this window - in my negligee - with a beer in my hand and I cough.

ANGELO. Cough? For what - what are you talkin' about?

MAFIA. Cough. Like this...*(Coughs into the window.)* See...it fogs up.

ANGELO. Yeah. So, big deal.

MAFIA. And I write, real fast, b'fore the fog fades away: "Be Happy."

ANGELO. *(Shakes his head from side to side, knowing what is coming next. SHE is going into one of her many self-pitying moments.)* Here's forty bucks.

MAFIA. *(Not looking at him.)* No.

ANGELO. What?!

MAFIA. I wait each dusk for 'em.

ANGELO. ...Who you wait for?

MAFIA. For the men to come home from work.

ANGELO. I don't wanna hear it.

MAFIA. There's one.

ANGELO. You want this? *(Meaning the forty dollars.)*

MAFIA. *(waves)* No. I want all of it.

ANGELO. All of it?!

MAFIA. All of it.

ANGELO. What about me?

MAFIA. Linger.

ANGELO. What?!

MAFIA. *(Shouts at the window.)* Linger, honey, linger, in the twilight. Stand on the stoop, at the bottom step, ignore the cold, honey, linger.

ANGELO. Ma?

MAFIA. Mafia - the name if Mafia. Look up here, honey, that's right...

ANGELO. What are you doing?

MAFIA. Now, that you've gotten yer look - take a walk...

ANGELO. What do you get outta teasing these assholes?

MAFIA. What I put in it. Satisfaction.

ANGELO. You get called a "cock-tease".

MAFIA. Coming from an asshole, it's not much of an insult. The asshole always gets screwed. You should know - this broad - whatever her name is - gave you a screwing.

ANGELO. Nobody screws me.

MAFIA. Oh, no?

ANGELO. Nobody.

MAFIA. I want all yer money.

ANGELO. I give you all my money - I ain't gonna have

any money—

MAFIA. That's right.

ANGELO. I ain't gonna have nothin' for myself.

MAFIA. Nothing but a single smile. The smile of a good deed. What is it they say? "Smile, and the whole world smiles with you." Do you believe that?

ANGELO. I'm gonna give you an extra ten. How's that? You got $50.

MAFIA. Smile.

ANGELO. I don't feel like smiling.

MAFIA. Refusing yer mother a smile.

ANGELO. I don't like smiling.

MAFIA. You want me to smile?

ANGELO. Do I want you to smile?

MAFIA. I wanna smile.

ANGELO. For what?

MAFIA. Smile and the whole world smiles with you.

ANGELO. Yeah, I know, you awready said that.

MAFIA. I wanna crack yer face with a smile.

ANGELO. Why?

MAFIA. I hate you.

ANGELO. I love you.

MAFIA. Gimme all yer money.

ANGELO. I hate you.

MAFIA. I love you.

ANGELO. I'll give you another ten - so you got sixty, awright?

MAFIA. I don't wanna argue about money...it's my "Happy Hour." *(Takes a beer out of the refrigerator - stands by the window.)* Open this. *(Hands him the beer. Does not look at him.)* Open it gently. The POP sound - twitches my hips, and I might all of a sudden forget where I am and start to strip.

ANGELO. *(Glares at her.)* What's wrong with you - are you flippin?

MAFIA. *(Still not looking at her son.)* Leave yer money on the table.

ANGELO. Or - are you being mean?

MAFIA. My beer. *(Extends her hand out to him - does not look at Angelo. ANGELO hands her the beer.)*

ANGELO. I'm leaving sixty dollars.

MAFIA. No! All of it - or nothing. *(ANGELO is frustrated - exhales heavily.)* Ammonia. It's the smell of ammonia. The Super must of just mopped. The Super always when he mops the building - starts from the top floor - from this staircase here - that leads to the roof. And he works his way down. Ammonia, ugh. Supers. The super Super. Me and him sat...the landing was cold and damp then. My skirt was raised and hugged the shaped of my hips - like an alligator sandwich bag. You see, baby, I was a virgin. And this guy knew it...His eyes...anxious - raised my skirt up to my waist. And I wondered. Wondered how will he spread my legs apart? Will he take 'em like he takes a wish-bone - and pull 'em apart? Or is he gonna get on one knee and wear my panties away by scraping with his teeth - words of love. "I love you," *(Sharply, boldly, saucily.)* Money, honey. Gimme some money! I really didn't think...Something done so fast - in the blink of an eye - On yer mark, get set, go!...Something done so quick- ...didn't even work up a sweat - Got offa me - didn't turn around to look back...Coulda gotten me pregnant!

ANGELO. Are you talkin' about me?

MAFIA. I couldn't see—

ANGELO. Look at me.

MAFIA. ...nothing ahead of me - except my pointed belly. *(MAFIA finally looks at Angelo.)*

ANGELO. Just what I needed to hear.

MAFIA. Don't tell me you didn't know.

ANGELO. I knew.

MAFIA. So what's wrong with hearing it from the horse's mouth?

ANGELO. I don't like the way you're saying it...Like yer trying to hurt me.

MAFIA. Yeah, it does seem that way. Not outta love - but outta love for money.

ANGELO. Thank you for tellin' me how I was born.

MAFIA. I screamed. Gamblin' with the throw of the dice. Seven - the winner - a baby boy. Craps the loser. A girl. *(Growls, shaking her fist as if she held in her hands a pair of dice.)* Seven - give mama - a pair of baby shoes...SEVEN!! The winner!...I won. Believe it or not - I won. Down in the gutter. I had you.

ANGELO. ...You want all my money?

MAFIA. *(pause)* I want it - and more.

ANGELO. *(long pause)* I've know you.

MAFIA. *(very noble)* You know me.

ANGELO. Yeah, so it's no surprise.

MAFIA. You know how I am.

ANGELO. I know.

MAFIA. This is the way I've always been.

ANGELO. I know.

MAFIA. An' you've known me to be worse.

ANGELO. With people - yeah.

MAFIA. What do you mean - with people?

ANGELO. With other people, not with me.

MAFIA. ...Well...it's rough.

ANGELO. On who?

MAFIA. *(shocked)* On who?

ANGELO. You - or me?

MAFIA. On me...of course.

ANGELO. Not me?

MAFIA. Mira - you? the cash they threw on the stage was not for me - but for you! You took every penny - You tellin' me it was rough living - like a king? I served you hand and foot!

ANGELO. Awright - forget it.

MAFIA. Yeah, how easily we forget.

ANGELO. I'm sorry.

MAFIA. Don't let me say - I'm sorry.

ANGELO. What do you mean?

MAFIA. I'd be sorry for a lot of things. *(Long pause. Steadying him. Her tone changes. Strutting like a sport.)* D'you think I'm worth the price of a ticket? Worth everything you have in yer pocket?...C'mon...Not as yer mother - But as a woman - I'm still...Splendid in black garters. Soaked in sweat - black garters that snap - stinging - faces with twisted grins, and crooked smiles. *(shouts)* MAFIA! Look, but don't touch - boys...*(quietly)* You can touch.

ANGELO. ...Why should I touch you?

MAFIA. 'Cause you want to. Why did you come down to the clubs and watch me - perform? 'Cause you wanted to. Like everybody there - you like what you saw. *(Long pause. ANGELO is shaken by her remarks. HE is speechless.*

MAFIA advances. Sensuous.) Here. Touch.

ANGELO. Who do you think I am? You don't know me.

MAFIA. I know you - You came outta me.

ANGELO. You don't know me.

MAFIA. You waz to be my knight in shining armor.

ANGELO. You don't know me.

MAFIA. You was my knight—

ANGELO. Stoppit.

MAFIA. In shining armor.

ANGELO. You don't know me.

MAFIA. *(defeated)* I no longer want to know you. *(SHE pauses. Then, in a sudden change of mood.)* God! Dammit! What do you want from me?...You seen me - like no son has seen his mother...We're not mother and son...

ANGELO. What are we? *(Studying her.)*

MAFIA. *(A glimmering of truth spreads across her face like a smile - and sparkles in her eyes. Awkward silence. SHE dramatically takes hold of both his hands and caresses her face with them.)* What are we?

ANGELO. I'm gonna slap this shit outta you.

MAFIA. Go 'head. Do whatever it is you have to do. *(SHE has his hands around her neck.)* But leave me all yer money on the table. That's how much it's gonna cost you. All of it. Every cent you have. *(SHE places his hands on her chest.)* I don't want to see you again. I don't want to see you up here. I don't like being left behind - here. It's terrible awful the way you don't lift a finger for me. *(No response from ANGELO. MAFIA edges towards him. Long silence. Places his hand on her breasts. Awkward silence.)*

ANGELO. *(in deep thought)* ...You know? Just the way

you're standin' there—

MAFIA. I'm not just standin' here.

ANGELO. I know. *(long pause)* I know...*(long pause)* You remind me of someone.

MAFIA. The woman - you loved...Loved to see on stage. *(shouts)* Mafia!

ANGELO. No.

MAFIA. Mafia!

ANGELO. No.

MAFIA. Mafia!

ANGELO. Virgin. *(MAFIA shoves him back violently.)* What the hell is wrong with you?! Are you jealous?

MAFIA. Depends on your intentions.

ANGELO. I wanna marry her.

MAFIA. For what?

ANGELO. I love her.

MAFIA. For what?

ANGELO. For what?!

MAFIA. I'll give it to you.

ANGELO. *(Angry. Long pause.)* You're gonna gimme it...

MAFIA. Whatever it is you want from her...

ANGELO. I want her.

MAFIA. You don't want her. You want what you always wanted. *(Slowly, for effect.)* When you first squashed yer cigarette butt on the floor - and stood alongside the other men sitting at the bar—

ANGELO. I knew—

MAFIA. You knew - when you looked up between my legs - You wanted me. I'm a woman - don't you think I can tell by jus' lookin' at ya?

ANGELO. You're my mother.

MAFIA. I love you.

ANGELO. *(long pause)* Don't make me say some things I'm gonna regret. Please - don't make me talk.

MAFIA. I wish you would.

ANGELO. I don't wanna.

MAFIA. Do it. I want you to—

ANGELO. No.

MAFIA. Yeah - it makes it easier to hate you.

ANGELO. ...I don't like—

MAFIA. I don't care.

ANGELO. I don't like—

MAFIA. I don't care. I don't care.

ANGELO. *(pause)* I don't like - disliking myself.

MAFIA. I don't care.

ANGELO. *(Displeased. Daring.)* ...I think of you all the time...

MAFIA. Good.

ANGELO. All the time.

MAFIA. Very good!

ANGELO. Naw, it's...I got you on my mind for all the wrong reasons.

MAFIA. Go 'head, say 'em...I wanna hear 'em...

ANGELO. ...It's not about you...It's about me. *(No response from MAFIA.)* ...I been puttin' myself down so much - I got heel marks on the back of my neck.

MAFIA. Good.

ANGELO. *(long pause)* Yer right.

MAFIA. Yeah.

ANGELO. 'Cause yer fuckin' right about everything.

MAFIA. *(smirking)* Uh-huh...Mother is always right.

ANGELO. But how come...You know...It don't affect you? Knowing...Knowing it - knowing I wanted to—

MAFIA. You want to...Not - wanted to - but still want to. You still want to!

ANGELO. *(long pause)* I use to always have dreams about you.

MAFIA. You still do.

ANGELO. I had a...a picture of you - a colored photograph of you dressed in yer...what do you call it?

MAFIA. In my pasties and G-string.

ANGELO. Yeah.

MAFIA. And you did what with it? What did you do alone with my picture?

ANGELO. *(Shakes his head from side to side. Solemnly. Bewildered. Frightened at what may happen - or be said next - but determined to forge ahead under his own steam.)* I'm gonna tell you this is...this is low life shit. This goes against everything. *(Sudden change in mood.)* Yeah...I want to. But I won't! I won't. I'm a lot of things. I'm a whole lotta things...I committed some nasty looking sins—

MAFIA. But you're not a "Motherfucker."

ANGELO. Here. *(Goes into his pocket.)* You want all my money?...Here. *(Puts all his cash on top of the kitchen table.)*

MAFIA. Is that all of it?

ANGELO. Yeah.

MAFIA. Are you sure? *(pause)* I want it all—

ANGELO. I gave you all of it.

MAFIA. That's not what I'm saying. I want it all - I don't wanna leave a penny for you to split in two - no. For what? So you can give the half that should by all rights be going to me - to some broad?! No - I want my half. But since you don't see it that way - I'm taking it - taking it all. This mother and son relationship is terminated.

ANGELO. We were never mother and son.

MAFIA. I'm exhausted.

ANGELO. We were never mother and son.

MAFIA. I'm tired of expecting - something.

ANGELO. We were never mother and son.

MAFIA. Anything. Even you on top of me - I'm willing to go that far - anything is better than nothing. It beats a blank. I'm sick. I'm sick. Sick and tired...

ANGELO. We were never mother and son.

MAFIA. I wish I could die. *(Turns on Angelo.)* SHUT-UP!

ANGELO. I never cared for you. I love you 'cause you're my mother. But I never cared for you.

MAFIA. We are all - all of us are born in a strange fashion - so what is yer hang-up?

ANGELO. I don't care about you.

MAFIA. That's why there is a God...for that reason. So we can all look up to him. *(SHE shouts.)* Help me - God - my son don't care about me!

ANGELO. ...I'm glad. Man, I'm fuckin' glad you're taking all my money. It proves, it proves - it proves what it was all about - "Money." I was kinda like an investment! I was gonna, gonna...

MAFIA. Reciprocate. The word is—

ANGELO. The word is nothing. I was - right?

MAFIA. I don't know what you was. You was a five dollar misunderstanding...You came cheap. How much you got there on the table? Looks like a couple of hundred dollars...Not bad for a five dollar invenstment.

ANGELO. I hate you.

MAFIA. *(Teasing, smiling.)* I love you...Look at all this money. *(Counts the money. Jubilantly. Relishing the moment.)* Lookit all these twenties. Wow! *(SHE stops counting the money. Stares down at it. Ponders for a moment. An uneasy silence prevails. Sneering - SHE deliberately takes each bill and one after the other throws it at Angelo's face.)* How's it feel? How does this feel?! Huh?

ANGELO. ...No different.

MAFIA. How's it feel to have it thrown in your face?! *(SHE continues to throw the money in his face. Increases the force with which she flings the money at him.)*

ANGELO. I feel the same. It feels the same way it always felt.

MAFIA. You love it!!

ANGELO. It hurts...

MAFIA. It doesn't hurt enough.

ANGELO. No.

MAFIA. *(SHE smacks him.)* How's that?!

ANGELO. *(A heavy silence. A thought strikes him. Looks at Mafia intently.)* You...You went in to work on days you didn't have to.

MAFIA. I had to.

ANGELO. No.

MAFIA. Yes.

ANGELO. You had it off with pay.

MAFIA. So?

ANGELO. You didn't have to go in.

MAFIA. *(evades)* You're steppin' on one of my

twenties.

ANGELO. Why you go in?

MAFIA. It's my job.

ANGELO. 'Cause you liked yer job.

MAFIA. You're still steppin' on one of my twenties.

ANGELO. You liked yer job.

MAFIA. Move your foot!

ANGELO. You was the star. *(MAFIA stoops and begins to pick up the money.)* Mafia!...My mother...It played tricks with my mind. It was nice - You bigger than life - It was something else, for a kid, it was a hell of a sight. I didn't know any better. I thought it was Hollywood. Showbiz. As a man...it was too late...I didn't care...I didn't care...I got the feelin' - if you were to hit the Lotto you'd still be down at the club. You were in control - Mafia!

MAFIA. I had 'em by all their balls. What do you think? Sure, I was in control.

ANGELO. Mafia - huh?!

MAFIA. Lift yer foot.

ANGELO. Then it's true - huh - what I said?

MAFIA. It's true - so what?

ANGELO. *(exhales heavily)* I always thought.

MAFIA. Move yer foot - I want to pick up my twenty.

ANGELO. I always thought I'd - been seeing things. Imagining things. Maybe...the guy I saw you kiss was an old-time friend of yours. Or - the guy who was feelin' you up - maybe he was a long lost relative or something. And not a guy who jus' walked in - an asshole who dropped in for a beer and a peek.

MAFIA. Lying to yerself - softens the blow - when you

keep telling 'em to yourself enough times. Move yer foot.

ANGELO. Yeah, whatever you say.

MAFIA. Move!

ANGELO. ...The night you didn't move. The night you had noodles for legs - and you had to leave all yer tips on the stage - 'cause yer legs got so trembly - Everybody had to take their drinks off the bar - or, else you woulda shooked 'em off - that's how bad—

MAFIA. *(With great force.)* Fucked up.

ANGELO. You was. Yeah...

MAFIA. Lift yer foot - c'mon!

ANGELO. It was then I knew nobody would ever hire you to dance again.

MAFIA. I'm still beautiful.

ANGELO. Yeah...Yeah...After all them years of shuffling you around in my head - with yer bad feet and aching legs, having my back patted like if I was yer man. "She's some woman!" Grinning when I was losing my mind...After all that I was gonna ask - for more by putting my head on the chopping block. Getting a job as a super in one of these tenement buildings here in the Bronx. So I could get free rent and put some kinda roof over yer head.

MAFIA. I want a house!

ANGELO. ...Yeah...But a house ain't in me. It ain't in you. Don't you know what I'm saying? We belong right here - where we are...You danced yer last dance. You had yer times of fellin' outta sight. And you had enough troubles to fill a dozen eight foot graves. You gotta face it - it's gotten away from us. We the last of the big time losers.

MAFIA. You're a loser.

ANGELO. Instead of investing yer money in me - you shoulda put it away somewhere for yer house.

MAFIA. I blew a lot of money on you.

ANGELO. You did. And I'm doing my best to pay back a little of it.

MAFIA. I want it all back - every cent of it.

ANGELO. I can't do that.

MAFIA. You owe me.

ANGELO. I think I've given you enough.

MAFIA. No.

ANGELO. I'm gonna take this twenty.

MAFIA. No, you're not. That twenty is mine.

ANGELO. I'm gonna use it for cab fare.

MAFIA. Not my twenty.

ANGELO. I'm gonna try to get as far away from here as I can.

MAFIA. I don't care where you go - as long as you keep sending me money.

ANGELO. I'm not gonna send you no more money. I'm gonna live, man. You got food stamps to live. You're collecting welfare. You got Medicare. I got to hustle for every buck I put in my pocket.

MAFIA. Good.

ANGELO. I hate you.

MAFIA. I hate you, too. *(Long silence. SHE moves back towards the stove, where SHE will take from behind it a large carving knife. Menaces him with it.)* You're not gonna take my twenty dollars.

ANGELO. Lend me it.

MAFIA. No, you walk.

ANGELO. Lend me it - O.K.?

MAFIA. No. *(Long silence. HE stoops down to pick up the twenty dollars. SHE rushes at him and stabs Angelo with the knife. The knife falls to the floor. ANGELO groans. MAFIA laughs hysterically. ANGELO slowly stands in pain - approaches her.)*

ANGELO. I was gonna send you money. *(MAFIA laughs.)* I was gonna send it. I wasn't gonna do something like that to you. You're my mother. *(MAFIA continues to laugh. ANGELO smacks her hard. The force of it knocks her over near the exit, where SHE falls. The audience only sees her bare legs. SHE is now in the exact position she was in the beginning of this piece. MAFIA continues to laugh loudly and to sob faintly. After concentrated attention, ANGELO approaches her.)* Here's yer twenty dollars. *(Drops the twenty-dollar bill at her feet. MAFIA, still laughing and sobbing, proceeds to rip the twenty-dollar bill. SHE will also tear to shreads the rest of the money. Her sobbing will increase louder and louder. Crosses over to the refrigerator - looks to side of it and removes a baseball bat.)* I hate you. God I hate you. I hate you so fuckin' much. *(Turns, advances, lifting the baseball bat high above his head. The ACTION FREEZES. The LIGHTS all will dim out, except for a SPOTLIGHT on ANGELO. HE will drop the baseball bat and will fall to his knees crying. To the audience.)* Poppa Dio!...

SLOW BLACKOUT

EPILOGUE

Darkness. As the HOUSE LIGHTS come up slowly, we hear the faint sounds of a BABY LAUGHING, and also hear the wonderful SOUNDS OF STREET LIFE.

A young MAN shouts, "Watch the car!"
A WOMAN sternly says, "Don't cross the street."
A passing BUS is heard.
WHISTLING. A car will honk its HORN. CHILDREN laugh. Police SIREN is heard in the far distance. All will come together and build to a climax.

Silence.

We are where we began in the Prologue.

The stage is littered with garbage. Miller beer bottles. El Diario newspaper is scattered. Empty food stamp booklets. Cans of Goya Beans are everywhere. In the center of the stage will be a wooden milk crate.

Entering is PAPO. HE stops, and faces the exit.

PAPO. What? Yeah. Uh-huh... I'm sorry too, she's a good woman... I don't know — I don't know how she is... The same... I'm waiting to hear something from the hospital. Dona Louisa is gonna lemme know as soon as they call her. *(Pause.)* Excuse me? *(Smiles, embarrassed.)* Did I eat something?... No, no I didn't eat nothing. Nah, no, don't do that. Thank you. Thank you. Oh, God! *(He is handed a paper plate of chicken and yellow rice.)* I love to eat. Does anybody want some? *(HE crosses to doorway.)* I'm lissening. Shush. *(Long silence.)* I'm lissening for Doña Louisa's phone. *(Inhales heavily.)* I don't know what I'm gonna do if I hear my mother died... She looks so old, white hair. *(Breaks down crying. Stops immediately. Does not look at the audience.)* This here is my world... I share it only when you and I exchange glances. *(Looks at the audience menacingly.)* When you and I brush up against each other—in the subway. Or, when I enter your neighborhoods to get a little of yer world. A taste of your world to take back home—back to the "Loisada" ... A color TV. Money. In some cases we take a life. *(A long silence.)* In my case when we lose a mother. We all need a mother. But I need one more than you. I'm sorry—that's the way I feel. *(Lost in thought.)* This person who is involved in the theatre said to me—when I said I had written this trilogy about people like myself—said to me, "Who cares?" I almost believed it. But anger stopped me... With two words, this person dismissed me. Broke my sword in two and flung it in my face! Solved my problem by denying I exist. Yes, I am a problem. I'm your problem—you're mine... I use to be into hating people. Nice people like yerselves I hated—I hated yous 'cause yous were comfortably miserable when I was just plain miserable. I hated anyone who had all the comforts of home—radiating offa them like a neon sign at the liquor store— Revolting—right? That's the way I felt when I looked at anyone who didn't resemble me. And that's the way some of you feel right now—when you look at me. I know you're tired. You

didn't think I'd notice—huh? We are communicating
and don't even know it... I'm learning about the world.
Having stepped outta this one—helped. My mother
dying—stopped me. You lissening—stopped me. I don't
wanna kill. *(Long silence.)* No. I want my mother to live. I
want to like people. And I wanna go back into my world.
This one right here. There is goodness here... I don't
know what good I can do... *(A long silence.)*

OFF-STAGE VOICE (FEMALE). Papo?

PAPO. What? Yeah?

OFF-STAGE VOICE. Tu mama.

PAPO. *(Panics.)* Oh, God, no. *(Covers his ears.)* I know
what you're gonna say... I know, I know, I know. She
died. *(Begins to swing the cane wildly.)* She died. My
mother... *(Breaks down, crying hysterically.)*

OFF-STAGE VOICE. *(Urgent.)* No, no, no. She's fine, she's
fine. They're going to send her home.

PAPO. *(Covers his face.)* Oh, God, thank you. *(Cries. HE
stops. Looks at the audience and smiles warmly. The LIGHTS gently come down on him.)*

BLACKOUT

PROP INVENTORY

Black netting w/assorted garbage (Prologue)
5 empty Miller beer bottles w/candles (A I)
2 large votive candles (1-A I, 1-A II)
1 empty "Gran Foder" votive candle (Prologue)
Pail of assorted garbage containing used syringes & cig-
      arette butts & paper plate w/chicken bones & white
      bread (A I)
Grey footlocker w/bloody rags (A I)
Coffee mug ¼ full of water (A I)
Maxwell House Coffee can w/syringe & rubber surgical
      tube (A I)
Bath tub (A II & III)
Rubber mat (A II)
Sm. palette of toilet supplies (A II)
Rug (A II)
Stove (A II & III)
Large pot (A II)
2 pot holders (A II)
Clock: set at 3:45 (A II)
Act II window curtains (Light & Bright)
Sink (A II & III)
Red dish rack (A II)
Garbage bag w/8 page section of local newspaper (A II)
Refrigerator (A II & III)
Statue of Sacred Heart Of Jesus (A II)
Sm. plate w/plastic apple (A II)
Telephone bill in envelope (A II)
Bottle opener (A II)

2 dish towels (1-A I, 1-A II)
Note to Raisin (A II)
Bottle of Malta w/cap (A II)
Wall phone w/50 ft. cord (A III)
White plate (A III)
Fork, bread knife (A III)
2 carving knives (A III)
Bed (A III)
Pile of dirty dishes (A III)
Large plastic garbage pail w/trash (A I)
Ironing board (A III)
Hair brush (A III)
Eyeliner (A III)
Cologn atomizer (A III)
Lipstick, nail polish (A III)
Bird cage (A III)
Shelf unit for fridge (A III)
Bottle of sleeping pills (A I)
Jack knife, keys on ring, sm. rubber ball (A I)
Money Totals: $1.00 (11), $10.00 (21), $20.00 (12), $5.00 (1)
Cooker (bottle cap) w/bobby pin (A I)
Dime bag of coke (A I)
Trick matches (tops of matches cut off, tips painted white, flashpaper put behind matches) (A I)
Red shoe laces (A II)
Playboy Magazine (distressed) (A II)
Kitchen broom (A II)
Plate for chicken (A III)
Wash cloth (A III)
Towel w/assorted ladies underwear (A III)

Assorted coins (A III)
2 plastic cups (A III)
Baseball bat (A III)
Act II kitchen table & 2 chairs
2 place mats (A II)
Salt & pepper shaker, ashtray (A II)
Sm. cabinet w/assorted kitchen items, can of Raid
    (A II)
Act III kitchen table, 2 matching chairs, 1 mismatch
    chair
Act III window shade, window is closed in III
Hanging ornaments
Napkins in holder
Tea kettle, pan w/cover, ashtray, enamel pot for rice
    (A III)
Lg. spoon, hot chocolate tin, sm. ashtray w/coins
    (A III)

ASSORTED SET DRESSING:
Grey ratty material (A I)
Gold frame, white feather (A III)
Palettes, black tights on hangar, dressing robe, (A III)
Basket w/assorted novelles & empty beer cans (A III)

PERISHABLES:
Book matches, sm. box of rosebud matches (as needed)
2 liter bottles of Pepsi & ginger ale (as needed)
Candles, paper towels, peanut butter cups (as needed)
Marlboros, Merits, Kool packs, watermelons (as needed)

PROPERTY AND FURNITURE SETUP

ON STAGE:
Black netting with assorted garbage on it.

ON STAGE LEFT:
Grey ratty material in window slats. Sm. box of Rosebud matches with 1 out (on window ledge).

ON STAGE RIGHT:
Medium tin can in wall to hold a candle with 2 book matches.

OFF STAGE LEFT:
2 empty Miller Beer bottles with candles, 1 large votive candle, pail of assorted garbage, also included in that is a plate of chicken bones & white bread & 2 cups of cigarette butts.

PROPERTY SETUP FOR SET PIECES:
Wall with bathtub: rubber mat on upstage end of tub
Palette of toilet supplies with rug draping around tub—
    downstage side (Act II)

Wall with kitchen appliances: Stove: large pot w/ 2 pot-
    holders
Clock on wall set at 3:45
Window: open with Act II curtains

Sink: red dish rack on top—underneath—garbage bag
with a section of 8 pages of a local newspaper (to be
spread out on floor).
Refrigerator: on top—statue of the Sacred Heart of Jesus,
large votive candle, sm. plate w/plastic apple, telephone bill in envelope, bottle opener, dish towel (on
door handle), note to Raisin to do his homework (on
fridge door), inside fridge—bottle of Malta (Pepsi) with
cap on it.
All of this setup is Act II.

Additional (Act III) wall units: One has a wall phone with
a 50 foot cord.
The other wall unit is a bed unit. Preset on it are: Ironing
board palette (assorted clothing in a heap), Refrigerator
palette (radio, toaster, nailpolish, cigarettes & matches),
Sink palette (dishrack w/assorted dishes, paper towels,
white plate, Italian bread in wrapper, fork, knife, carving
knife, cigarettes & matches, pile of dirty dishes.
Bath tub palette (assorted toilet items that are disarrayed)
Garbagebag palette (assorted bags bunched together)
Cigarettes & matches on bed

UP STAGE CENTER:
In the Act I wall unit is a large plastic garbage pail
with trash.
Behind the Act I wall unit for Act III is: an ironing board
w/a dress on a hanger, hairbrush, eyeliner pencil,
woman's cologne atomizer.
Small table w/assorted makeup items including lipstick
and nailpolish.

Birdcage
Shelf unit to go over refrigerator w/assorted items

OFF STAGE PROP TABLES:
ALLEY BOY:
        Bottle of sleeping pills
        1 Reeses Peanut Butter Cup in wrapper
        Jack knife
        Keys on key ring
        Small rubber ball
        3—$1.00/ 1—$10.00/ 1—$5.00

RANDY:
        Cooker w/bobby pin
        Dime bag of coke
        Real & trick matches
        Kool pack w/8 Merit cigarettes
        3—$1.00

LOOK OUT:
        3 Merit cigarettes

Watermelon: used in Act III, is wrapped up in a plastic
garbage bag and put into a pillow case.

Red shoelaces, distressed *Playboy* magazine (Raisin)
Bottle of Miller Beer (ginger ale) (Chino)
Kitchen broom (Raisin)
Plate w/chicken & yellow rice (Papo)

Can of Miller beer, wash cloth, dish towel, towel w/

assorted ladies underwear, Money: 5—$1.00/ 12—
$20.00/ 20— $10.00 (this is for Angelo), assorted coins,
cigarettes & matches, 2 plastic cups (one with warm
water, one with cold water), dressing robe, gold frame,
white feather, black tights on hanger, baseball bat, carving knife, basket w/assorted novellas & empty beer
cans.

OFF UP STAGE LEFT:
Act II kitchen table w/2 place mats, salt & pepper shaker,
ash tray.
Small cabinet w/assorted kitchen items & can of Raid on
top of cabinet: a mat w/compote
2 Act II kitchen chairs on table.

Act III kitchen table (wooden, oval)
2 matching wooden chairs, 1 mismatched chrome &
padded chair.

Preset on Act III table: Act III window shade, hanging
ornaments, napkins in holder, pack of cigarettes, wet &
dry book matches, teakettle, pan w/cover, ashtray,
enamel pot w/rice & spoon, tin of hot chocolate, small
ash tray w/coins.

PROP SETUP

PROLOGUE

PAPO
Aluminum cane
Switchblade

SOUTH OF TOMORROW (ACT I)

Tin coffee can w?
  Hyperdermic syringe
  Red plastic cord
Coffee mug—¼ full of water
4 candles in bottles
Small box of matches

RANDY
Dime bag
Bottle cap w/bobby pin
3 $1 bills
Carleton cigarettes
Matches (book)

ALLEY BOY
Bottle of pills
Reeses Peanut Butter Cups
Uniform donor card
Brush
Wallet
Pocket knife
Marlboro cigarettes

Matches (book)
$5 bill
3 $1 bills
$10 bill

DEALER
Cigarettes
Matches

NIJINSKY (ACT II)
Statue—on top of refrigerator
Telephone bill in envelope—on top of refrigerator
Dishrag—next to sink
Bottle of beer—in refrigerator
Playboy magazine—offstage of Right door
Broom—Raisin
Bottle of Miller beer (open) — in paper bag

POPPA DIO (ACT III)
Large pot w/rice
Small pot w/beans
Lid for small pot
Cooking spoon
Carving knife
2 plates
Washcloth
Dish towel
Radio
Can of beer
Marlboro cigarettes
Matches

Ashtray
Baseball bat
Telephone
Fork/knife

ANGELO
Marlboro cigarettes
Matches
Wad of money
Keys

EPILOGUE

Paper plate w/
  Chicken
  Yellow rice
Milk crate
Loose change

COSTUMES

RANDY
Tan polyester shirt (distressed)
T-shirt (distressed)
Cord pants (distressed)
Sweaters (distressed)
Army field jacket
Tan socks

ALLEY BOY
Short blue denim jacket (distressed)
Burgundy hooded sweat shirt
Jeans (distressed)
Sneakers (distressed)

RAISIN
Tie-dyed blue cotton T-shirt
Light yellow cotton jeans
White sweat socks
White sneakers
Apron with bib (floral)

CHINO
Pink-green print cotton shirt
Green cotton pleated slacks
White socks
Beige slip-on shoes

ANGELO
2 pc. grey-purple double-breasted suit
Maize & red stripe shirt
Grey-purple tie
Grey hanki
Black shoes
Black socks

MAFIA
Rose-colored 40's rayon dress with floral pattern
Black lace bra

PAPO
Black leather coat
Blue silk shirt
Black jeans
Black hi-heel boots
Cross & rings

THE VOICE
2 pc. black (satin-look) running suit
Black silk socks
Black suede shoes
Black hair scarf
Cross

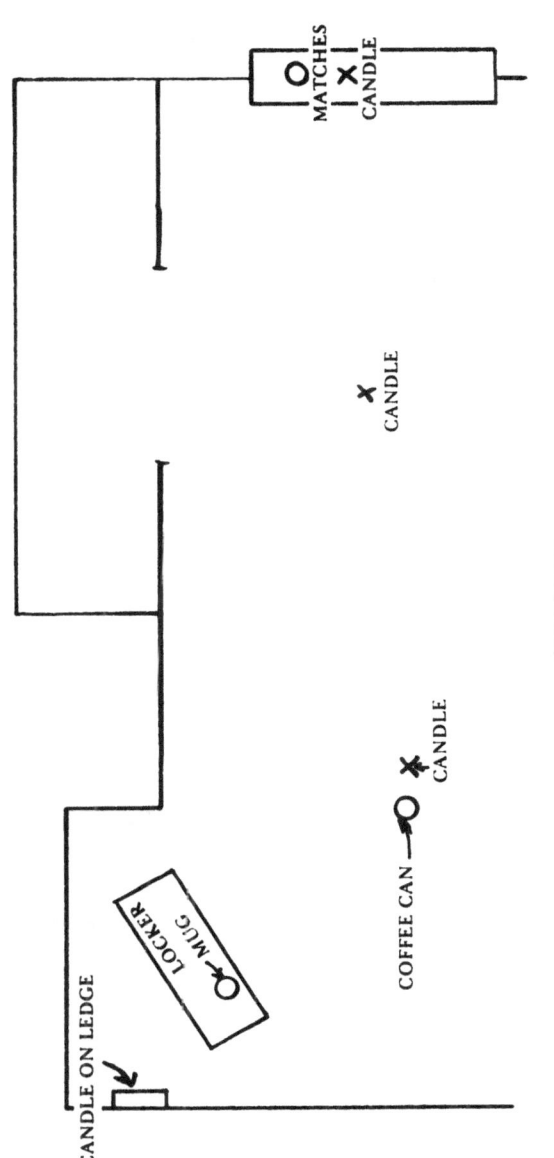

MATCHES

CANDLE

CANDLE

CANDLE

COFFEE CAN

CANDLE

LOCKER

MUG

CANDLE ON LEDGE

SET DESIGN
SOUTH OF TOMORROW

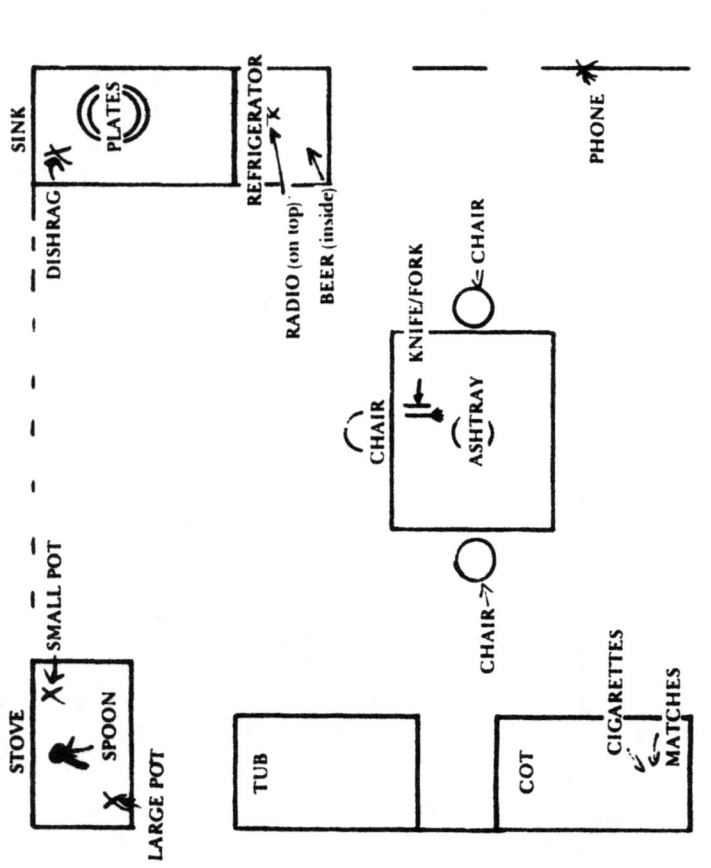

SET DESIGN
POPPA DIO

REINALDO POVOD

... was born and raised on the Lower East Side of New York City. He won the Oppenheimer/ *Newsday* Award for *Cuba and His Teddy Bear*, which starred Robert DeNiro, Ralph Macchio and Burt Young on Broadway. His second play, *La Puta Vida*, was given a reading at the Sundance Institute Playwrights Laboratory in the summer of 1985. Mr. Povod is the recipient of the Whiting Foundation Award. He dedicates this trilogy of plays to his grandmother, Lilia Esther Povod.

FOR COLORED GIRLS WHO HAVE CONSIDERED SUICIDE ...WHEN THE RAINBOW IS ENUF
Ntozake Shange

7f / Bare Stage

This groundbreaking "choreopoem" is a spellbinding collection of vivid prose and free verse narratives about and performed by Black women. Capturing the brutal, tender and dramatic lives of contemporary Black women, For Colored Girls... offers a transformative, riveting evening of provocative dance, music and poetry. Premiered by the Henry Street Settlement, Joseph Papp's Public Theatre and later on Broadway.

"A triumphant event, filled with humor. Pure theatre."
- New York Daily News

"A poignant, gripping, angry and beautiful work."
- Time

THE OFFICE PLAYS
Two full length plays by Adam Bock

THE RECEPTIONIST
Comedy / 2m., 2f. Interior

At the start of a typical day in the Northeast Office, Beverly deals effortlessly with ringing phones and her colleague's romantic troubles. But the appearance of a charming rep from the Central Office disrupts the friendly routine. And as the true nature of the company's business becomes apparent, The Receptionist raises disquieting, provocative questions about the consequences of complicity with evil.

"...Mr. Bock's poisoned Post-it note of a play."
- New York Times

"Bock's intense initial focus on the routine goes to the heart of *The Receptionist's* pointed, painfully timely allegory... elliptical, provocative play..."
- Time Out New York

THE THUGS
Comedy / 2m, 6f / Interior

The Obie Award winning dark comedy about work, thunder and the mysterious things that are happening on the 9th floor of a big law firm. When a group of temps try to discover the secrets that lurk in the hidden crevices of their workplace, they realize they would rather believe in gossip and rumors than face dangerous realities.

"Bock starts you off giggling, but leaves you with a chill."
- Time Out New York

"... a delightfully paranoid little nightmare that is both more chillingly realistic and pointedly absurd than anything John Grisham ever dreamed up."
- New York Times

www.ingramcontent.com/pod-product-compliance
Lightning Source LLC
Chambersburg PA
CBHW070622120726
47909CB00004B/1286